W9-BKT-159

Masters of the Dew

by

Jacques Roumain

Translated by

Langston Hughes and Mercer Cook

With an Introduction by J. Michael Dash

Masters of the Dew, Originally published in French as "Gouverneur de la Rosée" in 1944.
Author: Jacques Roumain.
Translation by: Langston Hughes and Mercer Cook

©Copyright 2017, Caribbean Studies Press an imprint of Educa Vision, Inc.

All rights reserved. No part of this book may be reproduced or transmitted in any form or by any means, electronic or mechanical, including photocopying, recording or by information storage or retrieval system except by a reviewer who may quote brief passages in a review to be printed in a magazine or a newspaper without permission in writing from the author.

For more information, please contact:
Caribbean Studies Press
2725 NW 19th Street,
Pompano Beach, FL 33069
Telephone: (954) 968-7433
E-mail: caribbeanstudiespress@eathlink.net
Web: www.caribbeanstudiespress.com

Library of Congress Control Number: 2016961790
ISBN 13: 978-1-58432-849-0 Cat. #: CSP 5739

Table of Contents

Introduction

Biographical Note

Jacques Roumain was born in Port-au-Prince in 1907 and came from an old wealthy Haitian family. He received his early education in Port-au-Prince and, as was expected for members of the elite in Haiti, was sent to Europe to complete his education. The influence of this cosmopolitan background would be evident in his later years. His work can be neatly divided into three periods: The American Occupation (1927-1936), Exile (1936-1940), Return and death (1941-1944).

1927-1936

Roumain returned to Haiti from Europe when he was twenty years old. At that time the American Occupation of Haiti, which had begun in 1915 and was to last nineteen years, was facing increasing hostility from the Haitian people. Roumain immediately took a violent nationalist and anti-American position and identified himself with a young iconoclastic generation of Haitians who formed the vanguard of the resistance movement. This radical group, of which Roumain became one of the leaders, was primarily responsible for the eventual end of the Occupation. The Nationalist cause gained momentum and matters were brought to a head by a student strike in 1929, which eventually turned into a general strike.

The position taken by Roumain and this "Generation of the Occupation" was twofold. In the first instance it was political in its violent nationalism but it also had wider cultural and literary implications. It was thought in the 1920s that Haiti should not only defend its sovereignty but should also create a strong and real cultural awareness. This gave rise to the "Indigenous" movement and Roumain became one of the founders of *La Revue indigene* (1927), in which a national literature based on an indigenous Haitian reality could find its expression. The ambivalence that existed among nineteenth-century Haitian writers as far as their indigenous culture was concerned was replaced by a militant indigenism, the aim of which was to make admissible in art a reality whose worthiness was once questioned. It was this unity of intention that distinguished Roumain's generation and was eventually to lead to the creation of novels like *Masters of the Dew.*

Roumain's position within the Indigenous movement was quite outstanding. Not only was he one of the most prolific members in the late 1920s but there were also two distinct features in his position that were apparent even at this time. Firstly, he refused to allow the ideology of Indigenism to become provincial and narrow. In the pages of *La Revue indigene* are numerous translations of the works of Latin American poets and the protest literature of the Harlem Renaissance movement in the United States. To Roumain, Indigenism was not simply a process of renaming and repossessing the Haitian landscape and the country's experience, it could also create an awareness of similar literary experiments elsewhere.

Indigenism was becoming increasingly preoccupied with the culture of the peasants in Haiti. In the 1920s and 1930s, inspired by the documentary work on peasant culture *Ainsi parla l'oncle* (1928) done by Jean Price-Mars, Haitian writers began to celebrate the rituals and customs of the folk. Roumain was among the first to respond to this desire to include folk material in his poetry. His *Sur le chemin de Guinée* for instance is based on the peasant belief that the soul after death returns to its ancestral home in Guinea. However, Roumain's distinguished himself in the early 1930s by a desire for objectivity, the second distinct feature of his position, which set him apart from many of his generation who were simply content to glorify and romanticize peasant culture.

The early prose works—*La Proie et l'ombre* (1930) and *Les Fantoches* (1931)—both depict Roumain's own class in Haiti. They show a parasitic elite trapped in its own prejudices of culture and class. This theme was naturally shared by other irreverent members of Roumain's generation who saw the traditional urban elite as a sterile class. Roumain, however, did not restrict his objectivity to this stratum of Haitian society. In 1931 the short novel *La Montagne ensorcelée* was published in which Roumain reveals a penetrating insight into the tragic reality of rural Haiti. This work goes beyond romanticizing the folk to present a chilling vision of how superstition and fear can produce tragedy. In the 1930s Roumain looked at these elements in Haitian society and saw in both cases stagnation and apathy.

It was at this time that Roumain saw Marxism as the way of explaining what had gone wrong in Haiti and as a possible solution for the problems that beset the society. He founded the Haitian Communist Party in 1934 and in the same year published his *Analyse schématique*, a Marxist analysis of Haiti's problems. The question of race and color was presented in terms of economic exploitation. Racial prejudice was simply "the sentimental expression of the class struggle, a psychological reaction to historical and economic circumstances." The class and color antagonisms in Haiti were explained in terms of Haiti's past:

> The parallel between the class structure of St. Domingue and the present Republic of Haiti is quite surprising. French

colonists and American Imperialists; the "affranchis" and the present day élite; slaves and the Haitian proletariat. . . .

The American Occupation and Marxist theory had thrown into sharp relief the pseudo-colonial nature of Haitian society. Marxism was to be the only ideology that Roumain could envisage as providing a genuine solution to the internal conflicts in Haiti. The attraction of Marxism for black writers was particularly strong in the 1930s. Langston Hughes, Richard Wright, and Aimé Césaire were drawn to the Marxist explanation of economic exploitation and the vision of a global proletariat.

In 1934 Sténio Vincent, then president of Haiti, reacted strongly against Roumain and the Communist Party. Roumain was arrested and imprisoned for three years for subversive activities. In 1936 he was released and sent into exile.

1936-1941

During his exile from Haiti, Roumain traveled widely in Europe. He began to study anthropology at the Sorbonne in Paris in order to acquire the necessary training to pursue his interest in peasant culture. Politically he was among those writers who tried to arouse the world's conscience over the tragedy of the Spanish Civil War. The poem *Madrid* written at this time reveals his idealism and the conception of an international fraternity struggling against Fascist domination.

At the outbreak of the Second World War, Roumain left for the United States where he began a long-standing friendship with Langston Hughes. He later visited Cuba where he spent a year with Nicolás Guillén whom he had previously met in Paris.

In 1939 he published his *Griefs de l'homme noir*, a Marxist analysis of the black American in the southern

United States. His analysis of racism and the phenomenon of lynching was based on the theory that racial prejudice was used as a divisive tool by the southern ruling classes to ensure that the poor whites and the blacks did not unify and change the order of things:

> The lyncher is also a victim of the lynching. The mobs that pursue the human "game" are composed of poor whites whose material condition is hardly better than that of the blacks. They labor under the illusion of white superiority and think they have something in common with the ruling classes. Color prejudice is a divisive tool among the workers of the South, whose common revolt could shake the established economic structure.

In 1941 Haiti elected a new president, Elie Lescot, who permitted Roumain to return to Haiti. The fact of the Second World War and Lescot's anti-Fascist stand also allowed Roumain to make his peace with the government of Haiti.

1941-1944

Immediately on his return to Haiti in 1941 Roumain founded the *Bureau d'Ethnologie* in an effort to legitimize the study of Haiti's peasantry. This organization was to devote itself to providing scientific monographs on the various manifestations of Haitian peasant culture, as well as Haiti's pre-Columbian past.

At this time Roumain once more found himself deeply involved in Haiti's intellectual life. The issue now centered around the "campagne anti-superstitieuse" waged by the Catholic church in an effort to convert all worshippers of the Vaudou deities. In 1942 Roumain published a long essay entitled *Autour de la campagne anti-superstitieuse* which reveals what he felt about this controversial religious campaign.

Roumain felt very strongly that Catholicism was no better for the peasants than Vaudou, in that the former did not essentially change their perception of reality. Vaudou to Roumain should not be persecuted. It should rather be viewed as the peasant dependence on the supernatural in order to explain his world, and consequently would only disappear when the peasant was provided with a scientific explanation of his reality. In the face of economic progress and enlightenment, the peasant would be more able to understand his world and control it. This was the only campaign that was worthwhile:

> The essential is not to make the peasant renounce his belief in Ogoun. It is rather a question of completely changing his conception of the world. . . . The element of moral coercion used in this campaign is fear. . . . But fear of hell fire has not radically changed their religious view of the world. They have not renounced their belief in the "loas" only their serving of these gods. . . . If one really wishes to change the archaic religious mentality of our peasants, we must educate them. And they cannot be educated unless their material conditions are transformed. Until we have developed a system of rural clinics, the peasant will continue to consult his "bocor" (priest). What we must have in Haiti is not a "campagne anti-superstitieuse" but a "campagne anti-misère."

As we shall later see, this attitude to peasant religion was central to Roumain's depiction of Vaudou and the religious mentality of the peasants in *Masters of the Dew*.

In 1943 President Lescot appointed Roumain chargé d'affaires at the Haitian embassy in Mexico. This job was accepted because of a directive from the Communist Party, which thought it was strategic to have famous Marxists placed in important public positions. It was a difficult decision for Roumain as he ran the risk of appearing to compromise himself politically.

It was in Mexico that he found the time to devote himself to creative writing which, in contrast to his early work, now reflects his Marxism. He completed the collection of poetry, *Bois d'ébène*, containing long declamatory poems which celebrated the fraternity and revolt of "les damnés de la terre" (the wretched of the earth). This line was to become the title of Fanon's famous work on the Algerian Revolution.

In early 1944 the manuscript for *Masters of the Dew* was finished. Roumain's own exile and return to Haiti is suggested in the experience of the character Manuel who in the novel returns from Cuba. The parallel between Roumain's creation of such a character and Claude McKay's creation of Bita Plant in *Banana Bottom* is quite striking. Both writers, because of their experience of exile, seemed to want to envisage in their creative imagination the possibility of returning to an environment in the Caribbean into which they could fit. Roumain's novel was published posthumously as he died very suddenly in 1944. It was considered a classic by most critics and eventually translated into a dozen languages.

A tremendous amount of activity seems to have been crammed into the seventeen years that followed his initial return to Haiti. It would have been interesting to see what path Roumain's Marxism would have taken in the 1950s (particularly after de-Stalinization in 1956) when numerous black writers defected from the Communist Party. Yet it was Roumain's achievement to have had the courage and insight to avoid the mystification of folk culture and examine with sensitivity as well as objectivity the question of national culture in a post-colonial society.

The Peasant Novel in Haiti

Masters of the Dew was by no means the first novel to treat a Haitian peasant situation. The particular literary genre of the peasant novel in Haiti goes back to the late nineteenth century. Roumain was certainly very conscious of the tradition in which he was operating, and the achievement of his own novel is revealed when it is placed in the context of the evolution of this genre.

The most striking feature of the Haitian peasant novel is that it is very different from the contemporary novel of the Third World that tends to be inspired by anti-colonial protest and the angst of the "assimilé" torn between the culture of the metropolis and that of his native land. From its first manifestation the peasant novel devoted itself to recording the experiences and survival of Haiti's peasantry in a post-colonial and national context.

The movements of Realism and Naturalism in France in the latter half of the nineteenth century were largely responsible for the birth of the Haitian peasant novel. The strong documentary and regionalist quality in the early Haitian novel was influenced by the metropolitan conception of the novel as a detailed record or, more precisely, a mirror of society. Man was no longer an abstraction but the product of a specific external environment. This theory of determinism led to the conception of the novel as a sociological investigation of the environment that determined and shaped the individual.

Along with this level of sociological investigation and photographic realism came the element of social consciousness. What Zola had done for the urban poor in France, the Haitian novelist wished to do for his peasantry. What was desired was more than local color. There seemed to be a need for a strong emotional commitment to exposing the harsh realities of peasant existence. In an essay published in 1903, Frédéric Marcelin wrote:

Think a little of these wretched, rural folk, cannon fodder for our political whims, for our passions, unwitting tools, play-things in our quarrels. We have ruined their fields, we have broken up and dislocated their humble families, we have in the end sent them to their deaths.

Two interesting peasant novels emerged from those published in this period. The first, *La Famille des Pitite-Caille* (1905) by Justin Lhérisson, is an interesting experiment of real originality in the novel form. Using a narrative framework drawn from the Haitian oral tradition, Lhérisson dramatically described in his modest vignette the adventures of a "nouveau riche" protagonist of peasant origins. His main character is mercilessly satirized in a mixture of Creole and standard French.

In 1906 Antoine Innocent published *Mimola*, whose story centered on the Vaudou religion. In this work we have descriptions of religious rituals so detailed that they verge on ethnography. This documentary quality is unfortunately included in a novel whose plot and characterization seem at times improbable and contrived. However, despite this lack of authority and assurance, at this time what we see is the beginning of a tradition that was later to yield as persuasive and accomplished a novel as *Masters of the Dew*.

Concern for Haiti's peasants and interest in the peasant novel were revived during the American Occupation because of the shortlived peasant revolt against the Americans. Charlemagne Péralte and his band of irregulars—called "cacos" and drawn from peasant communities—harassed the American marines for almost two years. This uprising was brutally put down and thousands of peasants killed. The tragic resistance of the peasantry immediately became an integral part of anti-American polemics.

The Indigenous movement and the popularity of Price-Mars' *Ainsi parla l'oncle* created widespread literary and artistic interest in the peasantry. This work severely criticized the cultural ambivalence of the traditional elite as regards the peasantry and encouraged the belief that the culture of the peasant was a valid source from which one could draw literary inspiration. This refusal to see peasant culture as hopeless and confining was a timely and necessary undertaking and responded directly to the identity crisis and the need for cultural authenticity which was posed by the Occupation.

It is in the context of this renewed interest in the peasant novel that Roumain and other members of his generation began to write about the peasantry. The direction taken by Roumain in his first short novel *La Montagne ensorcelée* is apparent when compared with the work of another novelist of the 1930s, Philippe Thoby Marcelin.

The latter tended to demonstrate in his fiction a strong regionalist tendency and an increasing penchant for the sensational and the exotic. In the novels *Canapé-vert* (1944) and *La Bête de Musseau* (1946) the reader is plunged into a world of mystery and the supernatural. Marcelin admitted to being influenced by an American study on Haiti, William Seabrook's *The Magic Island*, which dealt with sensational Vaudou rituals and cannibalism in Haiti. Marcelin's novels which set out to celebrate the culture of the folk in this manner could be no more than sensationalist and bizarre.

In contrast Roumain's novel showed a real attempt at reestablishing the link with the traditions of the peasant novel and eventually at providing new literary possibilities for it. Even Price-Mars' conception of peasant culture as part of "l'âme nationale" contained one important drawback—it tended to obscure and gloss over the grim realities of rural Haiti. Indeed, as far as the Vaudou is concerned, it underestimated the tragic potential of an excessive dependence on the supernatural. The members of the Indigenous movement who followed Price-Mars unquestioningly failed to give an objective picture of peasant culture and instead slipped into fantasy and melodrama in their work.

As we noted earlier, both authenticity and a social conscience were prerequisites among Haiti's novelists at the turn of the century. Roumain's work insists on both these features, and in *La Montagne ensorcelée* he goes beyond celebrating folk culture to present a moving account of how ignorance and superstition can be responsible for inhuman and irrational acts. It is a demonstration of the way in which peasant religion had become a spiritual refuge for the fears and insecurity of the peasantry. In this novel a small desolate peasant village is suffering from an interminable drought, and the inhabitants' only explanation is that they have been cursed by their gods. As the story progresses an old woman who lives apart from the villagers is suspected of witchcraft and blamed for their misfortunes. In order to rid themselves of their misery they resort to ritual murder. The old woman is stoned to death by a mob and her daughter beheaded.

The final scene of this novel expresses this chilling vision of human tragedy in the stunned reaction to the beheading of the daughter:

> The flash of the machette slashes down with a whistle, the head, severed, rolls on the grass.
> Everyone flees, except Balletroy who stares, his eyes empty, at the machette, the body, the body, the machette.

Sensationalism is controlled because the murder is seen as a blind irrational reaction to the misery and frustration that torment the villagers. In his vision of the limitations of peasant religion, Roumain was already indicating the ideological and artistic distance between himself and those who would blindly glorify the folk in the name of cultural authenticity.

The Achievement of *Masters of the Dew*

Over ten years after writing *La Montagne ensorcelée*, Roumain returned to this particular genre. In *Masters of the Dew* he revived themes and situations present in the earlier work, but this time the novel is conceived within an ideological framework. Instead of the total desolation and sterility of the earlier work we now see the possibility of a solution included in the depiction of the world of the Haitian peasant.

Roumain was tempted in *Masters of the Dew* to create a novel that would go beyond ethnographic detail and merely recounting events in Haiti's history. He conceived the peasant experience as a metaphor for a larger ideological and moral vision of humanity faced with destiny. In creating a wider resonance for his depiction of Haitian reality, Roumain belongs among those West Indian novelists who are conscious of the need to find an ideological or philosophical framework which could explain or interpret the West Indian experience. In this way, for instance, Orlando Patterson's *Children of Sisyphus* shows a similar combination of the particular and the universal.

In *Masters of the Dew* we return to the drought-stricken and desolate village of *La Montagne ensorcelée*. From the very beginning the dust and aridity of Fonds Rouge are emphasized, and as we are told later:

> They were worn out. The most reasonable among them were losing their senses. The strongest were wavering. As for the weak, they had given up. "What's the use?" they said. One could see them stretched out, sad and silent, on pallets before their huts, thinking about their hard luck, stripped of all their will power. (p. 82)

The use of alcohol, the desperate dependence on their Vaudou priests, their migration, all suggest a picture of sterility and resignation. Roumain projected his ideological vision onto this grim reality. It is interesting to note that the novel is not called *Fonds rouge* or *Manuel* but given a title that reflects the true nature of the author's intentions.

The original title *Gouverneurs de la rosée* (it would be difficult to find a genuine equivalent in English, and *Masters of the Dew* is as close as one could get) suggests three levels on which the novel was conceived. This title is firstly drawn from the peasant experience and a Haitian Creole expression meaning the peasant who sees about watering the fields. But more than being rooted in the peasant world, it suggests the Marxist conception of humankind as master of its own fate, imposing its will on the world. Thirdly, the use of "dew" rather than "water" provides a lyrical and poetic resonance to the experience described, suggesting behind the ideological message a universal kind of allegory.

The plot of the novel is quite straightforward. It concerns a young peasant, Manuel, who returns to his native village after working on a sugar-cane plantation in Cuba. On his return he finds his village stricken by a drought and divided by a family feud. He attacks the resignation endemic among his people by preaching the kind of political awareness and solidarity that he has learned in Cuba and goes on to illustrate his ideas in a tangible way by finding water and bringing it to the fields through the collective labor of the villagers. By merely considering the plot, one is tempted to reject the novel as another propagandist tract, and one critic was moved to dismiss it as "simply the inevitable Communist novel." However, Roumain is careful in this political fable to create an authentic environment and credible characters so that the work does not appear too contrived and ideologically manipulated. In the novel we are emotionally moved as well as ideologically persuaded.

Roumain does not make excessive demands on the reader's credibility because the illusion of reality created in

Masters of the Dew is carefully and persuasively established through the techniques of characterization and narration. The most obvious difficulty for a political novelist is the tendency for his characters to become nothing but "porte paroles" or ideological symbols. In his text Roumain permits a certain degree of individuality and autonomy to such secondary characters as Bienaimé and Délira, Manuel's parents. They are members of an older generation whose vision of the world is dramatically opposed to that of Manuel. The conflict between Manuel and his parents is symbolic of the antagonism between Manuel's ideas and those of Fonds Rouge. Yet we have a strong impression of these two characters not as one-dimensional puppets but as having distinct personalities. The following exchange between Délira and Bienaimé brings this out very clearly:

> But the old man insisted, "I tell you I'm a disagreeable Negro."
> "I know you inside and out. There isn't a better man anywhere."
> "You're contrary, *oui*, Délira! I swear I've never seen a more stubborn woman than you are."
> "Good, Bienaimé, that's right."
> "What's right, what?"
> "You *are* a disagreeable Negro."
> "*Me?*" said Bienaimé, disconcerted and furious. (p. 100)

Manuel, the chief protagonist, is unprecedented as a phenomenon in the peasant novel. He must have provided a challenge to Roumain's creative imagination because he is the source of the confrontation with tradition in the novel. Roumain is careful to create a character who even though intellectually more aware is emotionally and spiritually integrated into his community. Indeed,

Manuel in the novel straddles both the progressive and the traditional.

Two obvious examples of the integration of the hero into his community are his strong ties with his own culture and his relationship with Annaise. In the first instance Manuel's reaction to the Vaudou ceremony early in the book reveals that, in spite of his awareness of the essential futility of this ceremony, he cannot resist the overpowering effect of the various rituals:

> And Manuel, conquered by the magic beat of the drums in the depths of his being, was dancing and singing with the rest. (p . 46)

Manuel consequently tends to be less of an ideological abstraction and shows an inability to destroy old reflexes. Consistent with this sense of Manuel being rooted in his community and landscape is his strong feeling for nature:

> He wanted to sing a greeting to the trees: "Growing things, my growing things! To you I say, 'Honor!' You must answer 'Respect,' so that I may enter. You are my house, you're my country." (p. 34)

It is interesting to note that when Claude McKay in *Banana Bottom* is faced with a similar problem of reintegrating his heroine into her community, he resorts to identical techniques, even creating a situation in which she is similarly overpowered during a local religious ceremony.

Manuel's plausibility within the text is further reinforced by his relationship with Annaise. Through this relationship Roumain is able not only to expose other non-political qualities in his hero, but to modify any impression the reader might have of Manuel as a crusading revolutionary. For instance Manuel refuses the role of a messiah which Annaise wishes to attribute him:

> She   gazed at each of his features with extraordinary intensity, as if, slowly, he had been revealed to her, as if she were recognizing him for the first time. She said in a voice muffled by emotion, "Yes, you'll do it. You're the man who will find water. You'll be master of the springs, you'll walk through the dew in the midst of your growing things. I know you are right—and I know you are strong."
>
> "Not I alone, Anna. All the peasants will have a part in it, and all of us will reap the benefits of the water." (p. 67)

Later in their conversation we see Manuel not as the ideal proletarian hero but as an individual with very human and surprisingly modest ambitions. He sees himself in the role of Annaise's husband and enjoying a contented life in Fonds Rouge. There is no suggestion of a confrontation with the existing political authority in the novel.

The narrative technique serves equally to involve the reader in Roumain's peasant world. Conventional third-person narration or detached omniscience on the part of the author can create an impression of conscious didacticism in an ideological novel. Obvious authorial intrusion, for instance, can suggest that the novel is being manipulated toward a political end. What Roumain succeeds in doing in *Masters of the Dew* is reducing third-person narration to a minimum and presenting a text which seems to be narrated in the first person. Often in descriptive passages it is difficult to tell when the narrator stops and when the thoughts or fantasies of the characters begin. For instance, the novel begins with an objective description of Délira kneeling in the dust and almost imperceptibly the reader is plunged into the thoughts of the characters with an increasing use of the vocabulary and rhythms of the vernacular:

> But so many poor creatures call continually upon the Lord that it makes a big bothersome noise. When the Lord hears

it, he yells, "What the hell's all that?" and stops his ears. Yes, he does, leaving man to shift for himself. (p. 1)

Later in the novel at the wake for Manuel we have another instance of the same progression from objective description to a more subjective response to what is happening:

On each table, they had placed a candle that created the illusion of little islands of light in the yard. Peasants set around playing *trois-sept*. They held their cards like fans, and seemed absorbed. Had they already forgotten Manuel? Oh, no! You mustn't think that! (p. 145)

The reader consequently finds himself increasingly drawn into the world of Roumain's characters by the subtle blending of the narrative voice with those of the various characters.

It is onto this convincing picture of peasant reality that Roumain's Marxism is grafted. As is suggested in the title, the Marxist conception of humankind, not as alienated and passive but as master of the world, is pervasive in the novel. What Manuel is seeking to change is the peasants' conception of the world and their excessive dependence on the supernatural. The actual political implications of Manuel's position are never closely followed up and the inevitable confrontation with Hilarion and the Communal Magistrate is suggested at the end but never resolved. Roumain is more preoccupied with moral and philosophical ideals like the fraternity of the exploited and confidence in one's ability to control his/her world. The depiction of peasant religion clearly shows Roumain's ideological intention in the novel. The description of the effect of the Vaudou ceremony on the peasants indicates that Roumain is not interested in local color but in the narcotic effect such a ritual has on them:

Nevertheless the fête went on. The peasants forgot their troubles. Dancing and drinking anesthetized them—swept away their shipwrecked souls to drown in those regions of unreality and danger where the fierce forces of the African gods lay in wait. (p. 50)

Peasant religion, recognized as the product of ancestral traditions, is seen to have degenerated, however, into a desperate kind of retreat for the peasants. Manuel is painfully aware that the rituals of possession only produce an artificial paradise and such a temporary delirium cannot alleviate their continuing misery. He tells Annaise:

No, I respect the customs of the old folks, but the blood of a rooster or a young goat can't make the seasons change, or alter the course of the clouds and fill them with water like bladders. (p. 66)

Central to all that happens in Roumain's novel is the conflict between two visions of the world. It is within this conflict that Roumain's ideological position is defined.

The various elements that we have so far examined are neatly enclosed in a larger poetic framework, as has been seen in the very title of the work. Manuel's confrontation with Fonds Rouge is seen by Roumain in terms of a metaphor of a universal human situation. Beyond being a Marxist parable or an authentic evocation of peasant experience, Roumain's novel also operates on the level of universal poetic symbols. To this extent one can describe Roumain's technique as a kind of symbolic realism. This level of symbolism centers on the interplay of images of death and rebirth in the novel. For instance, the dust with its biblical associations of death and sterility is used to describe the spiritual and physical situation of Fonds Rouge. The overwhelming impression of barrenness and resignation is conjured up in the image of Délira kneeling in the dust at the beginning of the novel. This impression is maintained by Roumain with frequent reference to this image of decay as in "life had dried up in

Fonds Rouge" or "And one fine day, we fall into dust." The poetic importance of the water is thus established as the solution to this decay and is dramatically presented in the end as "a thin thread of water advanced, flowing through the plain...." The water suggesting the "dew" in the title becomes a symbol of potential and rebirth.

Another combination of symbols we find repeated is that associated with darkness and light. The dark with its associations of evil and a lack of vision is consistently used to describe the spiritual state of the village. For instance, the faces of the villagers sunk in their misery and divided by hatred are described as "dark unlighted walls." Comments such as "Fonds Rouge slumbered in the black night" strengthen this impression. Gervilen, who is the only wholly evil character in the novel, is presented as a deformed shadow—"a compact shadow, hardly different from the night" or later when Manuel is attacked, "a shadow danced before him...." In contrast to the associations of the dark, Manuel is consistently presented in terms of images of light. Délira constantly mentions the light on Manuel's forehead, and Manuel, before he is attacked, is seen holding a torch against the surrounding darkness. The light with its association of rejuvenation and a new vision is also closely associated with the coming of the water. The peasants dream of "Water! Its sunlit path across the plain." The end of the novel, which functions as a response to the first chapter (the desolation and aridity of the beginning contrasted with the theme of regeneration that is established at the end), further emphasizes this link between the water and the light. The savanna is described as "spread below them like an esplanade of violent light" in preparation for the water's arrival. In the original French, the coming of the water is presented in terms of an image of light, "une mince lame d'argent," which is not adequately translated by "a thin thread of water." Roumain obviously wished to retain the association of light with the water's arrival in order to suggest the renaissance that was now possible for Fonds Rouge.

From what we have seen of the complexity of Roumain's work, we can conclude that it is not a matter of forgiving Roumain for his good intentions as is sometimes the case with political art. Rather, what we see is a conscious manipulation of literary technique and conventions to create situations which have a firm grip on the reader's imagination. While never neglecting the legacy and resources of the peasant novel, Roumain was able to manipulate this genre even further to produce a parable of universal proportions.

Roumain's Use of Language and a Note on the Translation

In writing *Masters of the Dew* Roumain was obviously preoccupied with creating an authentic version of Haitian peasant reality as well as making it accessible to as wide a public as possible. Consequently, he sought to fashion a language that could serve these objectives of authenticity and accessibility.

Roumain accepted the basic thesis that there was a strong link between the language of a community and its experience. The retention of the Spanish "huelga" in Roumain's text is a simple example of his sensitivity to the relationship of language and experience. The notion of a strike is part of the Cuban experience and does not belong in the Haitian context. Consequently, there is no Creole word for "strike" and Manuel is forced to explain the meaning of the Spanish word. To this extent language edits the world and presents a people's perception of reality. This being the case, one could not avoid the use of Creole in the presentation of the Haitian peasant experience. This argument was accepted since the turn of the century as we have seen in Lhérisson's *La Famille des Pitite-Caille*. In order to be faithful to the peasant experience in his novel, Roumain had to create a language that was based on Creole but was accessible to a wide French-speaking public.

It is interesting to note that Roumain did not resort to slangy French or broken French in order to convey the characteristics of peasant speech. There is one occasion on which a version of broken French is used and is deliberately comical in its intention. Antoine's proposal to Sister Mélie is by no means his normal way of speaking and he tries to attain a false kind of elegance through the use of polysyllabic words and stilted expressions:

> I began in my Frenchest French. "*Mademoiselle*, since I seen you on the rectory porch, I had a passion of love for you. I've already cut poles, stakes and straw to build a house for you. On our wedding day, the rats will leave their rat holes and Sister Minnaine's baby goats will come and bleat in front of our door. So, to assure our authorization of love, *mademoiselle*, I ask your permission for a little effrontery." (p. 26)

Roumain's solution was to use both pure Creole words, many of which could be explained in footnotes or a glossary at the end, as well as a modified French which is not so much a translation as an adaptation of Creole. In Roumain's original text, songs, proverbs, and various interjections are left in Creole. There are also various words drawn directly from Creole which are retained such as "maringouin" (mosquito), "bayahonde" (acacia), "barranque" (ravine), and "grand-gout" (hunger).

Roumain's use of creolized French is more interesting and original. For instance such a linguistic combination becomes very necessary in the novel where the text slips into a first-person narration. For example, on the first page of the novel the movement from an objective description of Délira to an interior monologue is noted by a shift in vocabulary.

The English translation tries to make the movement more explicit by breaking it up into various paragraphs. In the original, from the moment we see "il y a tellement beaucoup de pauvres créatures qui hèlent le bon Dieu que ça fait un grand bruit. . ." we know by the shift to a more colloquial form of language that we have entered the protagonist's thoughts. Also in the direct speech of the characters we find a use of French which responds to the rhythms and syntax of Creole. For instance the following question asked by Annaise seems to retain the texture of Creole:

> Quel est ce grand causer que tu avais a me faire et comment, moi Annaise, je voudrais bien savoir, je pouvais aider un homme comme toi?

Consequently in the original text we find that the question of authenticity is strengthened by Roumain's creation of a language so heavily based on Haitian Creole. Roumain's linguistic achievement inevitably provides enormous problems for the translator. Literary translation is not merely a matter of making the text accessible to a wider audience but essentially a recreation of the author's world and indeed even an act of impersonation. To this extent the more specific and specialized the original work is, the greater the difficulty for the translator. In Mercer Cook and Langston Hughes we have a combination of talent which is seldom present in a translator. Hughes was not only a creative writer himself but had profound interest in the culture of the folk and both men had a real knowledge of the Haitian situation. Their failures and successes in translating this novel attest to the level and nature of Roumain's achievement.

In the English translation the vast majority of Creole words are translated into standard English, e.g. "mabouya" (lizard) and "maringouin" (mosquito). Only essentially untranslatable Creole words are retained, such as "coumbite," "houngan," and the names of the Vaudou deities. Cook and Hughes may have thought it artistically unsatisfactory to include too long a glossary at the end. In trying to find equivalents in standard English some of the atmosphere of the original had to be sacrificed. More often than not we sympathize with the problems of finding an appropriate translation for the vocabulary of Haitian Creole but there is one occasion where the need to find a literal English equivalent creates a serious error of judgment. The word "nègre" in Creole has lost all pejorative or even racial overtones and is best translated as "man" or "brother." Hughes and Cook have consistently translated it as "negro" often creating a very odd situation when it is used by the peasants.

We also find that the translators are sometimes torn between retaining the use of the Haitian flavor of the original and adapting Roumain's story to the language and situation of the rural southern United States. This sometimes creates an artificial combination of words drawn from both vernaculars. For instance, the Haitian use of "oui" as an interjection in certain statements is combined with the characters addressing each other as "honey" which suggests the rural South. However, there are certain occasions when the vernacular of the South is very appropriate to the atmosphere of the original. For instance expressions like "the earth's bad off," or "mighty funny," or "He didn't seem any too agreeable Bienaimé didn't" seem to approach what Roumain attempted in the original.

Since most of the difficulties in translating the text spring from Roumain's use of Creole, Hughes and Cook are most consistently successful in their ability to capture the lyricism of Roumain's standard French narrative. For example, the dust slipping between Délira's fingers is called a "rosary of pain" and Fonds Rouge waking up is described by "a light that can't make up its own mind, drowsy trees…." Roumain's ability to combine a strong realistic and lyrical quality in his style is caught in the description of the "coumbite" at the beginning. The following extract shows how the translators have preserved the prose poetry of the original:

> Suddenly the sun was up. It sparkled like a dewy foam across the field of weeds. Master Sun! Honor and respect, Master Sun! We black men greet you with a swirl of hoes snatching bright sparks of fire from the sky. There are the breadfruit trees patched with blue, and the flame of the flamboyant tree long smoldering under the ashes of night, but now bursting into a flare of petals on the edge of the thorn acacias. (p. 4)

The implications of Roumain's linguistic experiment are great for the Haitian peasant novel as well as for all Caribbean writers who strive after authenticity in their presentation of the experience and reality of the folk. It is perhaps not the only solution to the problem of using Creole in a literary context, but it certainly is one of the most successful experiments in this direction. As we have seen, the difficulty experienced by such capable translators as Hughes and Cook is evidence enough of the enormity of Roumain's technical achievement in this text.

Spatial Politics

In our analysis of the novel so far, we have treated Roumain essentially as a Haitian writer and activist. Yet Roumain can equally be seen in terms of the quintessential modern itinerant, diasporic intellectual. In this regard, he could be easily aligned with figures such as Frantz Fanon, Langston Hughes, W.E.B. Dubois, or C.L.R. James. What set him apart from the majority of his Haitian contemporaries was a life of exile and wandering as well as his ability to straddle diverse geographical and political spaces. His willingness to endure privation and estrangement from a world of privilege yielded a confident and creative capacity for intellectual work enriched by a range of scientific as well as humanist disciplines. Roumain's restlessness, his frequent dislocations are tied to many of his acute insights into understanding Haiti's positioning in a global context. For instance, it is not insignificant that *Masters of the Dew* was not written in Haiti but in Mexico where he had a diplomatic posting. Roumain at this point is not merely one of the outstanding products of Haitian Indigenism but very much a transnational intellectual with particularly strong links to anthropologists such as Paul Rivet with whom he had studied in France, the Swiss Alfred Metraux, the Cuban Fernando Ortiz, and the American Melville Herskovits. Not surprisingly the name of the protagonist of *Masters of the Dew* combines Latin American space with the biblical promise of a new beginning. Cuba is the crucial marker of Manuel's experience as a migrant worker and Spanish is made to supplement Creole with the language of worker activism that is missing in Haitian peasant speech.

Consequently, while the action of the novel is sited in an isolated Haitian village, Fonds Rouge is not on the margins but implicated in the warped space of a new economic order structured by global capitalism. As much as anything else, Roumain's novel is not just about the Haitian soul but a New World space in which the modern, materialist mind could emerge. Manuel is the incarnation of a new scientific, secular conception of knowledge based on observation and not tradition. The new model of knowing that he brings to Fonds Rouge is based on pragmatism and experience. Arguably the most revolutionary idea expressed in the book is suggested in his use of the Haitian saying "experience is the staff of the blind" in his conversation with Annaise. This is empiricism which in the context of Haitian peasant life undermines the kind of authority that is handed down and unquestioned. Manuel's heretical way of thinking defiantly usurps cherished assumptions of the limits of human agency and rural mastery of Haitian and hemispheric space. The gleaming knife edge of water that cuts through the landscape at the end symbolizes the victory of the experiential and the sensory, deliverance from the dust-clogged space of delirium graphically embodied by Délira Délivrance at the start of the narrative.

The pro-American politics of Haitian presidents after the end of the U.S. Occupation in 1934 made Roumain acutely aware that Haiti would continue to be vulnerable to foreign intervention and that little had been learned from the nineteen years of neo-colonial domination. In the period of forced exile in the 1930s and 1940s, Roumain shifts from the nationalist activism of the indigenist period to a Marxist-oriented focus on questions of labor in an international context. In this regard, he is more a cosmopolitan revolutionary like Frantz Fanon who in 1961 as we have seen, took the title of his last book, *The Wretched of the Earth* (*Les Damnes de la terre*) from Roumain's poetic call for proletarian revolt *Bois d'ebene*, published posthumously in 1945. In *Masters of the Dew* the move from the poetics of literary Indigenism to the politics of revolutionary ideology is neatly represented in the ritual of the coumbite as remembered by the aging Bienaimé and the renewal of this practice in terms of collective agency as envisioned by Manuel. The pastoral sentimentality of the former with its evidence of the retention of African practices gives way to the self-assured worker solidarity at the end of the novel where the huelga or strike that Manuel had witnessed in Cuba unleashes the potential for a cultural renewal of Fonds Rouge.

Little critical attention has generally been paid to the light-filled plain at the end of the novel but it constitutes utopian civic space whose open inclusiveness is precisely what is lacking in a Haiti where politics have moved indoors, into the authoritarian world of the national palace. Roumain's novel never mentions the capital or the palace but they both cast a long symbolic shadow over rural Haiti. The luminous plain is also opposed to the workers camp in which Manuel stayed while in Cuba. He explains to the inhabitants of Fonds Rouge shortly after his return that the land belonged to the Americans over there and that there were no peasants but workers. "I left thousands and thousands of Haitians over there in Antilla. They live and die like dogs" (p. 28). In these "bateys" for migrant workers, Manuel learns worker solidarity in a space outside of notions of private and public, citizen and alien since the camps are temporary sites for the displaced, perhaps not all that different from refugee camps. To compensate for the state of limbo in which these migrant laborers find themselves there is a profound sense of community. In his conversation with Annaise Manuel says

> At first in Cuba, we had no defense and no way of resistance… there were plenty of misunderstandings among us. We were scattered like grains of sand and the bosses walked on that sand. But when we realized we were all alike, when we got together for the *huelga*… (p. 68)

Through Manuel's experience in exile, Roumain makes a connection between displacement and self-invention. The workers camp in Antilla is not so much a place of loss but a stateless locale where the symbolic "dew" of renewal becomes possible.

The politics of *Masters of the Dew* are deeply utopian and oriented in terms of future promise. The novel conveys a speculative vision of a future unknown in the face of the stifled potential for change in the present. Nationalism and Indigenism were political dead ends by the mid-1940s. For Roumain the role of literature was to imagine alternative futures. It is the radical displacement and institutional terror of the workers camp that displaces Manuel from the consoling world of peasant values and establishes the ground for a radically new and modern consciousness. Forced to cohabit, to forge new worker alliances and to ultimately challenge the prevailing power structure Manuel lives a moment of quintessential global modernity. The politics of rural redemption in *Masters of the Dew* is anchored in the dislocating world of the batey where all past certitudes collapse and the dew of a new consciousness is secreted. In a deft fusion of the political, the religious, and the poetic, Roumain's protagonist has been made to enter the wretched underworld of U.S. capitalism and return to preach a gospel of new beginnings to a community incapable of even imaging a future beyond the unlivable present. Manuel is not so much the prodigal son but a version of Orpheus whose song is perpetuated after his death by Simidor Antoine. It is all summed up in the image of the pregnant widow, Annaise, at the end of *Masters of the Dew.* A future is waiting to be born as an old order had lost its legitimacy but the length of this richly symbolic gestation remains unclear as Annaise, like Haiti, is today still awaiting deliverance.

Chapter One

"WE'RE ALL GOING TO DIE," said the old woman. Plunging her hands into the dust, Délira Délivrance said, "We're all going to die. Animals, plants, every living soul! Oh, Jesus! Mary, Mother of God!"

The dust slipped through her fingers, the same dust that the dry wind scattered over the high hedge of cactus eaten by verdigris, over the blighted thorn acacias and the devastated fields of millet. The dust swirled up from the highway as the ancient Délira knelt before her hut, gently shaking her head covered with a gray frizz as though sprinkled with the same dust that ran through her dark fingers like a rosary of pain.

She repeated, "We're all going to die," and she called on the Lord.

But so many poor creatures call continually upon the Lord that it makes a big bothersome noise. When the Lord hears it, he yells, "What the hell's all that?" and stops up his ears. Yes, he does, leaving man to shift for himself. Thus thought Bienaimé, her husband, as he smoked his pipe, his chair propped up against a calabash tree. The smoke (or was it his white beard?) flew away with the wind.

"Yes," he said, "a black man's really bad off." Délira paid him no mind. A flock of crows swooped down on the charred field, like bits of scattered coal.

Bienaimé called, "Délira! Délira! Ho!" But no answer. "Woman!" he cried. She raised her head. Bienaimé brandished his pipe like a question mark. "The Lord is the creator, isn't he? Answer me! The Lord created heaven and earth, didn't he?"

Unwillingly, she answered, "Yes."

"Well, the earth's bad off, suffering. So the Lord created suffering." Short triumphant puffs and a long whistling jet of saliva.

Délira looked at him angrily. "Don't bother me, man! Don't I have enough trouble on my hands? I know what suffering is. My whole body aches, my whole body's full of suffering. I don't need anybody piling damnation on top of that."

Then, her eyes filled with tears, sadly, softly, "Bienaimé! Oh, honey!"

Bienaimé coughed hoarsely. Maybe he wanted to say something, but misfortune sickens men like bile. It comes up in their mouths, then the words are bitter.

Délira rose with difficulty, as if she were making an effort to pull herself together. All the trials and tribulations of life were etched upon her black face, but her eyes had an inner glow. Bienaimé looked away as she went into the house.

Back of the thorn acacias a hot haze distorted the half-hidden silhouette of far-off mountains. The sky was a gray-hot sheet of corrugated iron.

Behind the house a round hill, whose skimpy bushes hugged the earth, resembled the head of a Negro girl with hair like grains of pepper. Farther away against the sky, another mountain jutted, traversed by shining gullies where erosion had undressed long strata of rock and bled the earth to the bone. They had been wrong to cut down the trees that once grew thick up there. But they had burned the woods to plant Congo beans on the plateau and corn on the hillside.

Bienaimé got up and walked unsteadily toward the field. Dry weeds had invaded the bed of the stream. The watercourse was cracked like old porcelain, slimy with rotten vegetation. Formerly the water had flowed freely there in the sun, its rippling and its light mingling like the soft laughter of cutting knives. Then millet had grown abundantly, hiding the house from the road.

In those days when they all had lived in harmony, united as the fingers of the hand, they had assembled all the neighborhood in collective *coumbites* for the harvest or the clearing.

Ah, what *coumbites*! Bienaimé mused.

At break of day he was there, an earnest leader with his group of men, all hard-working farmers: Dufontaine, Beauséjour, cousin Aristhène, Pierrilis, Dieudonné, brother-in-law Mérilien, Fortuné Jean, wise old Boirond, and the work-song leader, Simidor Antoine, a Negro with a gift for singing, able to stir up with his tongue more scandal than ten gossiping women put together. But without meaning any harm, only for fun.

Into the field of wild grass they went, bare feet in the dew. Pale sky, cool, the chant of wild guinea hens in the distance. Little by little the shadowy trees, still laden with shreds of darkness, regained their color. An oily light bathed them. A kerchief of sulphur-colored clouds bound the summits of the mountains. The countryside emerged from sleep. In Rosanna's yard the tamarind tree suddenly let fly a noisy swirl of crows like a handful of gravel.

Casamajor Beaubrun with his wife, Rosanna, and their two sons would greet them. They would start out with, "Thank you very much, brothers," since a favor is willingly done: today I work your field, tomorrow you work mine. Cooperation is the friendship of the poor.

A moment later Siméon and Dorisca, with some twenty husky Negroes, would join the group. Then they would all leave Rosanna bustling around in the shade of the tamarind tree among her boilers and big tin pots whence the voluble sputtering of boiling water would already be rising. Later Délira and other women neighbors would come to lend her a hand.

Off would go the men with hoes on shoulder. The plot to be cleared was at the turn of the path, protected by intersecting bamboos. Creepers with mauve and white blossoms hung from riotous bushes. In their gilded shells the assorossis sported a red pulp like velvet mucous.

Lowering the fence poles at the entrance to a plot of land where an ox skull for a scarecrow blanched on a pole, they measured their job at a glance—a tangle of wild weeds intertwined with creepers. But the soil was good and they would make it as clean as a table top. This year Beaubrun wanted to try eggplant.

"Line up!" the squadron chiefs would yell.

Then Simidor Antoine would throw the strap of his drum over his shoulder. Bienaimé would take his commanding position in front of his men. Simidor would beat a brief prelude, and the rhythm would crackle under his fingers. In a single movement, they would lift their hoes high in the air. A beam of light would strike each blade. For a second they would be holding a rainbow.

Simidor's voice rose, husky and strong:

Stroke it in!

The hoes fell with a single dull thud, attacking the rough hide of the earth.

> *That woman said, man!*
> *Behave yourself!*
> *And don't touch me!*
> *Behave yourself!*

The men went forward in a straight line. They felt Antoine's song in their arms and, like blood hotter than their own, the rapid beat of his drum.

Suddenly the sun was up. It sparkled like a dewy foam across the field of weeds. Master Sun! Honor and respect, Master Sun! We black men greet you with a swirl of hoes snatching bright sparks of fire from the sky. There are the breadfruit trees patched with blue, and the flame of the flamboyant tree long smoldering under the ashes of night, but now bursting into a flare of petals on the edge of the thorn acacias. The stubborn crowing of cocks alternated from one farm to another.

The moving line of peasants took up the new refrain in a single mass voice:

> *Stroke it in!*
> *Who's that, I yell,*
> *Inside that house?*
> *Some man yells back,*
> *Just me and a cute*
> *Little cousin of mine—*
> *And we don't need you!*

They raised their long-handled hoes, crowned with sparks, and brought them down again with a terrific precision:

> *I'm in there now!*
> *Bring it out! Oh!*
> *What one bull can do,*
> *Another can, too!*
> *Bring it out! Oh!*

There sprang up a rhythmic circulation between the beating heart of the drum and the movements of the men. The rhythm became a powerful flux penetrating deep into their arteries and nourishing their muscles with a new vigor.

Their chant filled the sun-flooded morning. Up the road of the reeds along the stream, the song mounted to a spring hidden in the hollow of the hill's armpit, in the heavy odor of fern and moist *malanga* soaking in the shaded secret oozing of the water.

Perhaps a young *Négresse* in the neighborhood, Irézile, Thérèse, or Georgiana, has just finished filling her calabashes. When she comes out of the stream, cool bracelets ripple from her legs. She places the gourds in a wicker basket that she balances on her head. She walks along the damp path.

In the distance the drum sends out a humming hive-full of sounds.

"I'll go there later," she says to herself. "So-and-so will be there." He's her sweetheart. A warmth, a happy languor fills her body as she hurries on with long strides, arms swinging. Her hips roll with a wondrous sweetness. She smiles.

Above the thorn acacias floated tatters of smoke. In the clearings, the charcoal sellers swept away the mounds under which the green wood had burned with a slow fire. With the back of his hand, Estinval wiped his reddened eyes. From the mutilated tree there remained only the charred skeletons of its scattered branches in the ashes: a load of charcoal that his wife would take to sell in the town of Croix des Bouquets. Too bad he himself couldn't answer the call of the work-song! Smoke had dried his throat. His mouth was bitter as if he had been chewing a wad of paper. Indeed, a drink of cinnamon bark, or better, anis was more refreshing, a long big mouthful of alcohol down to the pit of his stomach.

"Rosanna, dear," he said.

Knowing his weakness, she laughingly measured out three fingers of liquor for him—three fingers spread out like a fan. He spat thick and went back to rummaging in his pile of earth and ashes.

About eleven o'clock, the call of the *coumbite* would grow weaker; it was no longer a solid mass of voices backing up the men's effort; the work-chant stumbled, mounted feebly, as though its wings were clipped. At times it picked up again, spasmodically, with diminishing vigor. The drum still stammered a bit, but it was no longer a happy call as at dawn when Simidor beat it out with such skillful authority.

This could be attributed not only to the need for rest—the hoe becoming heavier and heavier to handle, the strain of fatigue on the stiff neck, the heat of the sun—but to the fact that the job was almost done. Moreover, they had scarcely stopped long enough to swallow a mouthful of white rum, or to rest their backs.

The high-class people in the city derisively called these peasants "barefoot Negroes, barefooted vagabonds, big-toed Negroes." (They are too poor to buy shoes.) But never mind and to hell with them! Some day we will take our big flat feet out of the soil and plant them on their behinds.

They had done a tough job, scratched, scraped, and shaved the hairy face of the field. The injurious brambles were scattered on the ground. Beaubrun and his sons would gather them up and set fire to them. What had been useless weeds, prickles, bushes entangled with tropical creepers, would change now to fertilizing gashes in the tilled soil. Beaubrun was overjoyed.

"Thanks, neighbors!" he kept repeating.

"You're welcome, neighbor!" we replied, but hurriedly, for dinner was ready. And what a dinner! Rosanna wasn't a cheap *Négresse*. All those who had made little spiteful remarks about her—because she was an ugly customer if you tried to get fresh with her—straightway repented. And why? Because, at the turn of the road, an aroma rose to meet them, greeted them positively, enveloped them, penetrated them, opened the agreeable hollow of a great appetite in their stomachs.

And Simidor Antoine—who, not later than two evenings ago, on making a vulgar remark to Rosanna, had received remarkably precise details from her concerning his own mother's irregularities—filling his nostrils with the aroma of the meats, sighed with solemn conviction, "Beaubrun, old man, your wife is a blessing!"

In the cauldrons, the casseroles, and the bowls were stacked barbecued pig seasoned hot enough to take your breath away, ground corn with codfish, and rice, too, sun rice with red beans and salt pork, bananas, sweet potatoes, and yams to throw away!

Bienaimé leaned against the fence. On the other side now there was the same discouragement. The dust rose in thick swirling clouds, and fell on the chandelier trees and thin patches of grass clinging to the scurvy earth.

Formerly at this time of year, early in the morning, the sky would be turning gray. The clouds would gather, swollen with rain—not a heavy rain, no, as when the clouds burst like over-filled sacks—but a little drizzle, persistent, with a few intervals of sunshine. It wasn't enough to drench the earth, but cooled it off and prepared it for the hard rains. At Ángelus-time, the timid wild guinea fowl would come to drink water from the puddles along the road and, if frightened, would fly heavily away, benumbed and bespattered with rain.

Then the weather would begin to change. Toward noon, a thick heat would envelop the prostrate fields and trees. A thin mist would dance and vibrate. The sky would break out into livid blisters, which later on darkened and moved ponderously above the hills, splashed by flashes of lightning and echoing thunder.

Deep on the horizon, an enormous enraged breath. The peasants, caught in the fields, hurrying along with hoe on shoulder. The trees bent. Violently shaken by the now uninterrupted baying of the storm, a swift curtain of rain had overtaken them. At first a few warm unhurried drops, then, pierced by flashes of lightning, the black heavens had opened in an avalanche, a torrential deluge.

Bienaimé, on his narrow porch with its railing protected by a projecting thatched roof, would look at his land, his good land, his streaming plants, his trees swaying in the chant of the wind and rain. The harvest would be good. He had labored in the sun for days at a time. This rain was his reward. He watched it affectionately as it fell in close-knitted threads, he heard it splash on the stone slab in front of the arbor. So much and so much corn, so many Congo beans, the pig fattened. That might mean a new jacket, a shirt, and perhaps neighbor Jean-Jacques' chestnut colt, if he would lower the price.

He had forgotten Délira. "Warm up the coffee, wife," he would say. Yes, he'd buy her a dress and a madras, too. He filled his short clay pipe. That was what living on good terms with the earth meant.

But all that had passed. Nothing remained now but a bitter taste. They were already dead beneath this dust, in these warm ashes that covered what formerly had been life. Oh, not an easy life, no, indeed! But they had persisted, and after struggling with the earth, after opening it, turning it over and over, moistening it with sweat, sowing it with seed as one does a woman, then came satisfaction: plants, fruit, many ears of corn.

He had just been thinking about Jean-Jacques and here, coming along the road, was Jean-Jacques, as old and worthless now as he, leading a skinny burro and letting its cord drag in the dust.

"Brother," he greeted him. And the other answered the same.

Jean-Jacques asked for news of Sister Délira. Bienaimé said, "How's Sister Lucia?"

And they thanked one another.

The burro had a large sore on its back and winced under the bite of flies.

"*Adieu, oui,*" said Jean-Jacques.

"*Adieu,* old man." Bienaimé nodded.

He watched his neighbor plod on with his animal toward the watering place, that stagnant pool, that eye of mud covered by a greenish film, where all drank, men and beasts.

He's been gone so long, he must be dead now, she mused. Old Délira was thinking of her son, Manuel, who had left years ago to cut cane in Cuba. He must be dead now, in a foreign land, she thought again. He had said to her one last time, "Mama!" She had kissed him. She had taken in her arms this big fellow who had come from the depths of her flesh and blood, and had become this man to whom she whispered through her tears, "Go, my little one, may the Holy Virgin protect you!" And he had turned at the elbow of the road and disappeared. "Oh, son of my womb, sorrow of my womb, joy of my life, pain of my life! My boy, my only boy!"

She stopped grinding coffee, but remained squatting on the ground. She had no longer any tears to shed. It seemed to her that her heart had petrified in her breast and that she had been emptied of all life save that incurable torment that gripped her throat.

He was to return after the *zafra*, as the Spaniards call the harvest. But he hadn't come back. She had waited for him, but he hadn't come. Sometimes she would say to Bienaimé, "I wonder where Manuel is?"

Bienaimé wouldn't answer. He'd let his pipe go out. He'd walk away through the fields.

Later, she would again say to him, "Bienaimé, papa, where's our boy?"

He would answer roughly, "Hush your mouth!" She would pity his trembling hands.

She emptied the drawer of the coffee mill, poured in more beans, and again took the handle. It wasn't hard work, yet she felt exhausted. It was all she could do to sit there motionless, her worn-out body given over to death that would in the end bring her to this dust.

She began to hum. It was like a groan, a moan from the soul, an infinite reproach to all the saints and to those deaf and blind African deities who did not hear her, who had turned away from her sorrow and her tribulations.

"O, Holy Virgin, in the name of the saints of the earth, in the name of the saints of the moon, of the saints of the stars, of the saints of the wind, in the name of the saints of the storm, protect if it be thy will, I pray thee, my son in foreign lands! O, Master of the Crossroads, open to him a road without danger! Amen!"

She hadn't heard Bienaimé return. He sat down near her. On the side of the hill there was a dull redness as the sun sank behind the woods. Soon night would shroud the bitter earth in silence, drowning their misery in the shadow of sleep. Then dawn would rise with the husky crowing of cocks and day would begin again, hopeless as the day before.

Chapter Two

"STOP!" HE TOLD the bus driver.

The driver looked at him in amazement, but slowed down. Not a hut in sight; they were right in the middle of nowhere. There was only a stretch of thorn acacia trees, gum trees, and thickets strewn with cactus. A range of gray hills ran toward the east, fading into the sky.

The chauffeur put on the brakes. The stranger got off and pulled down a bag that he threw over his shoulder. He was tall, black, dressed in a high-buttoned coat and trousers of rough blue material caught in leather gaiters. A long, sheathed machete hung at his side. He touched the broad brim of his straw hat and the bus moved on.

Under a clump of juniper trees the man recognized an almost invisible pathway between a mass of rocks spurting stems of amaryllis bedecked in yellow blossoms. He inhaled the odor of the juniper trees, intensified by the heat. His memory of the place was linked to this peppery odor.

His bag was heavy, but he didn't feel its weight. He hiked up the strap that held it on his shoulder and started off through the woods.

"Ho!" he exclaimed as a stray cat leaped across the path, swerved suddenly, and disappeared in a sound of crushed foliage.

No, he had forgotten nothing. Now another familiar odor came up to meet him—the musty smell of stale charcoal smoke when all that is left of the pit is a circular mass of dirt.

A narrow, shallow ravine opened before him. It was dry. Tufts of weeds and all sorts of prickles had invaded its bed. The man raised his head toward a bit of sky soaked in hot steam, took out a red handkerchief, mopped his face, and seemed to reflect. He went down the path, scattering pebbles on the burning sand. Dead roots crumbled in his fingers when he examined the rough-grained earth, so dry that it trickled like powder.

"¡*Carajo!*" he cried.

He walked slowly up the other side, his face worried, but only momentarily. Today he had too much to be happy about. Water sometimes changes its course like a dog changes masters. Who knew where the vagabond was flowing now? He strolled toward a mound crowned with macaw trees. Their crumpled fans hung inert. There wasn't a breath of air to open them and turn them into a wild play of dazzling light. This was a detour for the stranger, but he wanted to embrace the countryside from above, to see the plain spread out before him and glimpse, through the trees, the thatched roofs and irregular blots of fields and gardens.

His face, drenched with sweat, hardened, for what he saw was a grilled expanse of dirty rusty color spotted by a scattering of moldy huts. He stared at the barren hill overlooking the village, ravaged by wide whitish gullies where erosion had bared its flanks to the rock. He tried to remember the tall oaks once animated with wood pigeons fond of blackberries, the mahogany trees bathed in shadowy light, the Congo beans whose dry husks rustled in the wind, the long rows of sweet potato hills. But all that, the sun had licked up, effaced with a single stroke of its fiery tongue.

He felt as though he had been betrayed. The sun weighed on his shoulders like a burden. He went down the slope into the savanna where emaciated cattle were wandering through thorny bushes searching for a rare blade of grass. Flocks of crows perched on the tall cactus flew away at his approach in a dark whirl of interminable caws.

Just then he met her.

She was wearing a blue dress gathered in at the waist by a foulard. The knotted wings of the white kerchief which held her hair covered the nape of her neck. Carrying a wicker basket on her head, she walked quickly, her robust hips moving in cadence with her long stride. At the sound of his steps she turned around without stopping, her face in profile, and she answered his greeting with a timid and somewhat uneasy, "*Bon-jour, m'sieur.*"

He asked, as if he knew her—for he had lost his manners—how she had been.

"By the grace of God, all right," she said. "*Oui.*"

He explained, "I'm from around here—from Fonds Rouge. I left this country a long time ago—fifteen years this Easter. I was in Cuba."

"Is that so?" she said weakly. She wasn't happy over the presence of this stranger.

"When I left, there wasn't any drought. Water ran in the ravine, not much, to tell the truth, but always enough to do, and sometimes even enough for a little overflow, if it rained in the hills." He looked around him. "Seems like it's been cursed now."

She answered not at all. She had slackened her pace to let him go by, but he gave her the path and walked on at her side. Furtively she stole a glance at him. He's too fresh, she thought, but she didn't dare say so.

Walking along without paying attention to where he was going, he stumbled over a big rock in the road and it took him several droll little jumps to regain his balance.

"Watch out," she cried, breaking into laughter.

He saw that she had lovely white teeth, frank eyes, and very fine black skin. She was a tall, well-built girl. He smiled at her.

"Is today market day?" he asked.

"Yes, at Croix des Bouquets."

"That's a big market. In the old days folks used to come from everywhere, everywhere on the way to that village on a Friday."

"You talk about the old days as if you were already old." She was suddenly startled by her own boldness.

Narrowing his eyelids as though he were watching a long road unfold before him, he replied, "It isn't time so much that makes you old, it's what you have to put up with in life. Fifteen years I spent in Cuba, fifteen years, every day cutting sugar cane, *oui*, every day, from sunrise to dusk-dark. At first, the bones in your back get all twisted up like a corkscrew. But there's something makes you stand it. What? Tell me, do you know what it is?"

He clenched his fists as he talked.

"It's being mad—that's what! Being mad makes you grit your teeth and tighten your belt when you're hungry. Being mad's a great power. When we went on strike, each man stood in line, armed to the teeth with being mad—like a gun. To get mad, that's your right, your justice!"

She hardly understood what he was saying, but she was completely absorbed in this somber voice that hit each sentence hard, and sometimes threw in the magnificence of a foreign word.

She sighed, "Jesus-Mary-Holy-Virgin! Life gives poor folks a hard road to go. *Oui*, brother, that's the way it is! There's no relief."

"Yes, there is relief, too! I'm going to tell you what—it's the earth, your own plot of land that you've cleared by the strength of your arms, with your own fruit trees around it and your own stock in the pasture, everything you need right there—with your own freedom bounded by nothing but the weather, good or bad, rain or drought."

"That's right," she said, "but this land doesn't produce anything anymore. When you've eked out a few sweet potatoes or a few grains of millet, they bring in next to nothing at the market. Life is a penance these days."

Now they were skirting the first cactus fences. In the empty spaces between the thorn acacias wretched huts crouched. Their worn-out thatch covered a thin layer of wicker plastered with mud and crackled whitewash. In front of one of these, a woman was crushing grain in a mortar, with the aid of a wooden mallet. She stopped, with suspended gesture, to watch them pass.

"Madame Saintélis, *bonjour, oui*," the girl cried from the road.

"Oh! *Bonjour*, my pretty Annaise, how're all your folks, my lovely *Négresse*?"

"Everyone's fine, thanks. And you?"

"No worse, no, except my husband, who's down with the fever. But that will pass."

"Yes, that will pass, my dear, with the Good Lord's help."

They walked a moment.

"So," he said, "your name is Annaise."

"Yes, Annaise is my name."

"Mine's Manuel."

They met other peasants with whom they exchanged greetings, and sometimes she would stop to pick up and distribute news, for in Haiti that's a neighborly custom. Finally, she came to a fence. There was a hut back in the yard under the shade of some logwood trees.

"This is where I live."

"I'm not going much farther either. I'm glad I met you. Will we be seeing each other again?"

She turned her head away, smiling.

"Since I live right in front of you, you might say," he continued.

"Really! Where?"

"Down there by the curve in the road. You must know Bienaimé and Délira. I'm their son."

She almost snatched her hand from his, her face convulsed by a kind of painful anger.

"Hey! What's the matter?" he exclaimed in Spanish. But she had already gone through the gate, moving rapidly without once turning around. For a few seconds he stood rooted to the spot.

"A funny girl, old man," he said to himself, shaking his head. "One minute she's smiling at you friendly-like, then before you can bat an eye, she leaves you without even, '*au revoir*'! What goes on in a woman's mind, not even the devil knows."

To put up a front, he lit a cigarette and sucked in the pungent smoke that reminded him of Cuba with the immensity of its cane fields stretching from one horizon to the other, the grinder at the sugar refinery, and the stinking barracks where, with the coming of evening after an exhausting day, he would lie down helter-skelter among his comrades in misfortune.

As soon as he entered the yard, a shaggy dog bounded toward him, barking furiously. Manuel pretended to stoop for a stone to throw at him. The dog ran off yelping, his tail between his legs.

"Quiet! Quiet!" old Délira called as she came out of the hut. She shaded her eyes with her hand, the better to see the stranger. He walked toward her and as he approached, a great light began to shine in her soul. She started to rush toward him, but her arms fell to her sides. She staggered and her head rolled back.

He pressed her to him. She buried her face on his chest. With her eyes closed, in a voice weaker than a breath, she murmured, "My baby! Oh, my baby!" Through her faded eyelids tears were flowing. She gave in to all the weariness of endless years of waiting, having no power now for joy, just as she had none for bitterness.

In astonishment, Bienaimé let his pipe fall. He picked it up and wiped it carefully on his jacket.

"Give me your hand, boy," he said. "You've stayed away a long time. Your mother has prayed at lot for you." He looked at his son, his eyes tear-dimmed. Then he added in a vexed tone, "Even so, you might have announced your coming, or sent a neighbor on ahead with the word. The old woman's nearly shocked out of her wits. You don't have much sense, son."

He felt the weight of his bag. "You're more loaded down than a burro!" He tried to relieve Manuel, but gave way beneath its weight and the bag almost fell. Manuel grabbed it by the strap.

"Leave it be, papa, this bag is heavy."

"Heavy?" Bienaimé protested, ashamed. "At your age I carried heavier ones than that. This young generation's spoiled, no strength! Worthless, I'm telling you, this young generation!"

He fumbled in his pocket for the wherewithal to fill his pipe. "Got any tobacco? In the country you've just left, they say tobacco's as common as bushes on our hills. To hell with those Spaniards, anyhow! They take our children away from us for years, and when they come back they've got no consideration for their old parents. What are you laughing about? Now he's laughing, the shameless rascal!" Indignant, he called Délira to witness.

"But papa," said Manuel, holding back a smile.

"There's no, 'but papa,' about it. I asked if you had any tobacco. You could've answered me, couldn't you?"

"You didn't give me a chance, papa."

"What do you mean—that I talk all the time? Do words fall out of my mouth like water through a strainer? So you want to disrespect your papa?"

Délira tried to calm him, but the old man pretended to be furious, and was enjoying it.

"I don't want to smoke now, you aggravate me too much! On the very day of your arrival, too!"

But when Manuel offered him a cigar, he took it, sniffed it with veneration, then feigned a grimace of displeasure.

"I wonder if it's any good. I like my cigars plenty strong, I do." Looking for an ember, he walked toward the shed-kitchen covered by dry palm leaves.

"Pay him no mind," said Délira, touching her son's face in a gesture of timid adoration. "He's like that. It's his age. But he's got a good heart, *oui.*"

Bienaimé returned. Now he had on his fair-weather face. "Thanks, son, this is a real cigar, all right! Say, Délira, why are you hanging on to that boy like a clinging vine?" He took a deep puff, looked at the cigar with admiration, expectorated with a long whistling spurt of saliva. "Yes, damn it! This is a real cigar, worthy of its name! Let's drink something to calm us down, son."

Manuel found the hut faithful to his memory: the little porch with its railing, the earthen floor paved with pebbles, the decayed walls through which one could see the wicker laths. Far back into the past he looked, and as he looked a wave of bitterness receded across those cane fields where the endless fatigue of broken bodies measured each day's toil.

He sat down—at home with his folks, back with his own—this rebellious soil, this thirsty ravine, these devastated fields and, on his own hill, that rough mane of vegetation standing out against the sky like a fractious horse.

He touched the old oak buffet. "*Bonjour! Bonjour!* I'm back!" He smiled at his mother as she wiped the glasses. His father sat with his hands on his knees, staring at him, even forgetting to draw on his cigar.

"Life's life," he said finally.

That's true, Manuel thought. "Life is life!" No need to take short cuts or make long detours—for life is a continual coming back. The dead, they say, come back to Guinea, and even death is only another name for life. The fruit that rots in the ground nourishes a new tree.

When under the flogging of the rural police he used to feel his bones crack, a voice would whisper, "You're still alive! Bite your tongue, swallow your cries! You're a man! When push comes to shove, you've got what it takes. If you go down, you'll be seed for an unending harvest."

"You damned Haitian! You black hunk of dung!" the police howled in Spanish.

But their blows didn't even hurt any more. Through a haze charged with lightning shocks, Manuel heard deep in his blood the never-ending call of life.

"Manuel?" His mother was serving him something to drink.

"You look as starey-eyed as a man seeing werewolves in broad daylight," said Bienaimé.

Manuel emptied his glass at a gulp. The alcohol, perfumed with cinnamon bark, caressed the pit of his stomach with a burning tongue as if its fire rushed to his veins.

"Thanks, mama. That's good *clairin*, and very warming."

Bienaimé drank in turn, after pouring a few drops on the ground. "You've forgotten your manners," he scolded. "You've got no respect for the dead. They, too, are thirsty."

Manuel laughed. "Oh! They don't have to be afraid of catching cold! Me, I've been sweating. My throat's dry enough to spit dust."

"You're impudent, all right—and impudence is what stupid Negroes think is being smart." Bienaimé's anger started to rise again, but Manuel got up and put his hand on his shoulder.

"A person would think you weren't glad to see me."

"I? Who said that?" The old man stammered excitedly.

"No, Bienaimé," said Délira to calm him, "nobody said that. No, papa dear, you have your fun and be happy. Our boy's here. The Good Lord has blessed us, given us consolation. Oh, thanks be to Jesus and the Virgin Mary! Thanks be to my saints! Three times over I thank you!" She was weeping. Her shoulders shook gently.

Bienaimé cleared his throat. "I'm going to tell the neighbors."

Manuel took his mother in his long muscular arms. "No more crying, please, mama. From today on, I'm here for the rest of my life. All these years I've been like an uprooted tree in the current of a river. I drifted to foreign lands. I looked hardships in the face. But I struggled until I found the way back to my own land. Now it's for keeps."

Délira wiped her eyes. "Last night, I was sitting here where you see me now. The sun had gone down. It was pitch dark already. Out in the woods a bird just kept on calling. I was afraid something was going to happen and I thought: Am I going to die without seeing Manuel anymore? You see, I'm old, baby son. I have pains, my body's no good anymore and my head isn't any better. Then, too, life is hard. The other day I was saying to Bienaimé, I was saying to him, 'Bienaimé, how are we going to make it? The drought's overtaken us, everything's wasting away, animals, plants, every living human. The wind doesn't push the clouds along any more. It's an evil wind that drags its wings on the ground like swallows and stirs up dust-smoke. Look at the swirls of dust on the savanna. From sunup to sunset, not a single bead of rain in the whole sky. Can it be that the Good Lord has forsaken us?' "

"The Lord hasn't got a thing to do with it!"

"Don't talk nonsense, son!"

Frightened, old Délira crossed herself.

"I'm not talking nonsense, mama. There's heavenly business and there's earthly business. They're two different things, not the same. The sky's the pastureland of the angels. They're fortunate—they don't have to worry about eating and drinking. Of course, they have black angels to do the heavy work—like washing out the clouds or cleaning off the sun after a storm—while the white angels just sing like nightingales all day long, or else blow on little trumpets like the pictures we see in church.

"But the earth is a battle day by day without truce, to clear the land, to plant, to weed and water it until the harvest comes. Then one morning you see your ripe fields spread out before you under the dew and you say —whoever you are—'*Me—I'm master of the dew!*' and your heart fills with pride. But the earth's just like a good woman: if you mistreat her, she revolts. I see that you have cleared the hills of trees. The soil is naked, without protection. It's the roots that make friends with the soil, and hold it. It's the mango tree, the oak, the mahogany that give it rainwater when it's thirsty and shade it from the noonday heat. That's how it is—otherwise the rain carries away the soil and the sun bakes it, only the rocks remain. That's the truth. It's not God who betrays us. We betray the soil and receive his punishment: drought and poverty and desolation."

"I'm not going to listen," said Délira, shaking her head. "Your words sound like the truth—but the truth's probably a sin."

The neighbors began to arrive, the peasants Fleurimone Fleury, Dieuveille Riché, Saint-Julien Louis, Laurélien Laurore, Joachim Eliacin, Lhérisson Célhomme, Jean-Jacques, the Simidor Antoine, and the good women, Destine, Clairemise, and Mérilia.

"Cousin," said one, "you stayed away a long time."

"Brother, we're happy to see you."

A third called him, "pal." They each took his hand in their big rough hands, the hands of tillers of the soil.

Destine, greeting him with a curtsy: "I'm not saying this as a reproach, but Délira was pining away, the poor woman!"

And Clairemise kissed him. "We're relatives! Délira's my aunt. The other day I told her one of my dreams. I saw a black man, a very old man. He was standing on the road where it crosses the path of macaw trees, and he said to me,

'Go and find Délira.' The rest I didn't hear. The roosters were crowing and I woke up. Maybe it was Papa Legba."

"Or else it was *me*," said Simidor. "I'm old and black, but the womenfolk still love me. They know that walking's better with old sticks. They see me even in their dreams."

"Shut up," said Clairemise. "You've got one foot in the grave and you're still running around."

Simidor laughed loud and long. He was broken and tittering like a tree with rotten roots, but he sharpened his tongue the livelong day on the whetstone of other folks' reputations, and he could tell you a pile of stories and gossip, without sparing saliva. He looked at Manuel with a spark of malice in the corner of his eye and revealed his few remaining snaggled teeth. "Excusing the expression, the proverb says, 'Urine that spreads don't foam.' But may the lightning cut me in two if *you* aren't a fine looking Negro!"

"He's always saying stupid things out in company," Destine chided. "Now he's cursing! You certainly had a bad upbringing!"

"Yes," said Bienaimé proudly, "he's a big strapping fellow all right. I recognize my blood there. Old age has stunted me, but in my youth, I was a head taller than he is."

"Délira," Mérilia interrupted, "Délira darling, I'm going to make you some tea to calm your nerves. You've had more than your share of excitement today."

But Délira was looking at Manuel, at his forehead hard and polished like a black stone, at his determined mouth which contrasted with the veiled and rather faraway expression of his eyes. Joy not unmixed with sorrow stirred in her heart.

"Good!" began Laurélien Laurore. He was a stocky peasant, slow in movement and in language. When he spoke, he clenched his fists as if to hold on to the thread of his words. "Good! I'm told that in the country of Cuba they speak a language different from ours, a jargon, you might say. I'm also told that they talk so fast you can open your ears wide without understanding anything at all, since each word is mounted on a four-wheeled carriage going full speed. Can you speak that language?"

"Of course," Manuel replied.

"Me, too!" Simidor exclaimed. He had just swallowed two drinks of white rum in rapid succession. "I've crossed the border several times. Those Dominicans over there are folks like us, except that they have a redder color than us Negroes of Haiti and their women are mulattoes with heavy hair. I knew one of those dames—big and fat, *Antonio*, she called me, yes, that's how she called me. Compared to the women over here, there wasn't a thing lacking. She had some of everything—and good, too! I could swear to that, but Destine would jump on me afterward. Destine, darling, it isn't the tongue that counts. No, it's what else you've got." He stifled a little hilarious cough. "Take my word for it!"

"I'm not your darling! You're a vagabond! A good-for-nothing!" Destine was beside herself, but everyone laughed.

"Antoine! What a man!"

The bottle of white rum went the rounds. Manuel watched the peasants as he drank, seeing in the wrinkles of their faces the deep marks of poverty. There they were around him barefoot, and, through the holes of their patched garments, he saw their dry earthy skin. All of them carried machetes at their sides, from habit no doubt, for what work was left now for their idle arms? A bit of wood to cut to repair fences, a few thorn acacias to chop down for charcoal that their wives would take on burro-back to sell in town. That was how they eked out their famished existence, adding the sale of poultry or, from time to time, a thin heifer exchanged for little or nothing at Pont Beudet.

But now they seemed to have forgotten their fate. Enlivened by alcohol, they were laughing at Antoine's inexhaustible chatter.

"Friends, I'm telling you—do I usually lie?—I say that that little *Négresse*, that Mamzelle Héloise, is getting rounder and rounder. That's what comes from playing games with young fellows. In my day, this problem of girls was more of a chore. We had to maneuver, pretend, speak French, cut all sorts of shenanigans and make all kinds of fuss. In spite of which, you still found yourself caught for good in the end and tied down like a crab with a hut to build and furniture to buy, not to mention dishes.

"Take Sister Mélie, for example. That devil could set a holy-water basin on fire. Smooth black skin, eyes with lashes of silk long as reeds, teeth just made for sunshine! Furthermore, round all over, nice and plump like I like 'em. Just look at her and the taste of hot pepper came to your mouth. When she walked her hips rolled clear down to the bottom of her dress. She'd make you lose your soul—and upset the marrow of your bones!

"One afternoon, I met Sister Mélie coming from the spring near Cangé's cornfield. The sun was going down—dusk-dark. Not a soul on the road. After talking and talking, I took Sister Mélie's hand. She lowered her eyes and said simply, 'Antoine! Oh, but you're fresh, *oui*, Antoine!' In that day and time, we were brighter than you Negroes are today. We had 'instriction.' So I began in my Frenchest French, '*Mademoiselle*, since I seen you on the rectory porch, I had a passion of love for you. I've already cut poles, stakes, and straw to build a house for you. On our wedding day, the rats will leave their rat holes and Sister Minnaine's baby goats will come and bleat in front of our door. So, to assure our authorization of love, *mademoiselle*, I ask your permission for a little effrontery.'

"But Sister Mélie took her hand away with her eyes sparkling. She answered, 'No, mussieu, when the mangoes bloom and the coffee ripens, when the *coumbite* crosses the river with drums beating, then if you're in earnest, go call on my papa and mama.'

"To eat, you've got to sit at the table—to get Sister Mélie, I was obliged to marry her! She was a good woman who died long ago. Eternal rest be hers! Amen!"

He gulped down an entire goblet of white rum in a single gulp. The peasants guffawed.

"What a rascal!" Destine whispered, curling her lips in scorn. But Laurélien Laurore, with a kind of patient determination on his placid face, kept on questioning Manuel.

"Good! I'm going to ask you something else. Have they got any water?"

"Plenty of it, old fellow. Water runs from one end of their plantations to the other, and it's good cane that's grown there, with a greater output than our Creole cane."

All were listening now.

"You could walk from here to town without seeing anything but sugar cane, sugar cane everywhere, except now and then some little old palmetto, like a forgotten broom."

"So you say they have water," said Laurélien thoughtfully.

Dieuveille Riché asked, "To whom does that land belong, and all that water?"

"To a white American, Mr. Wilson by name. The factory, too, everything all around is his."

"And the peasants, are there peasants like us?"

"You mean with a plot of land, poultry, and a few head of cattle? No, they're only workers who cut the cane for so much and so much. They've got nothing but the strength of their arms, not a handful of soil, not a drop of water—except their own sweat. They all work for Mr. Wilson, and this Mr. Wilson sits in the garden of his fine house all the time under a parasol, or else he's playing with other whites knocking a white ball back and forth with a kind of washerwoman's paddle."

"Eh!" Simidor said bitterly this time, "if work was a good thing, the rich would have grabbed it all up long ago!"

"That's right, Simidor!" Saint-Julien Louis approved.

"I left thousands and thousands of Haitians over there in Antilla. They live and die like dogs. *Matar a un Hatiano o a un perro*: to kill a Haitian or a dog is one and the same thing, say the rural police. They're just like wild beasts."

"That's a damn shame!" Lhérisson Célhomme exclaimed.

Manuel remained silent a moment He remembered one night when he was on his way to a secret meeting. They were getting ready for a strike.

"Halt!" a voice cried.

Manuel leaped to one side, backing into the shadows.

In spite of the rustling of the wind in the sugar cane, he heard, not far from him, someone breathing excitedly. Invisible, tense, he waited, his hands ready.

"Halt! Halt!" the voice repeated nervously.

A weak flash cut the darkness. But with one jump, Manuel seized the revolver and broke the policeman's wrist. They rolled on the ground. The man tried to call for help. With a blow from the butt end of the revolver, Manuel bashed in his teeth, striking ever harder until he sank the weapon deep into his flesh.

He sighed with satisfaction at the memory.

"Yes," Simidor said, "that's how it is. And it's wrong! The poor work in the sun, the rich play in the shade. Some plant, others reap. Certainly we ordinary folks are like a pot. It's the pot that cooks the food, that suffers the pain of sitting on the fire. But when the food is ready, the pot is told, 'You can't come to the table, you'd dirty up the cloth.' "

"That's exactly it!" cried Dieuveille Riché.

Sadness came over the peasants. The second bottle of *clairin* was empty. They were brought back to their own plight and to the thoughts that tormented them—drought, ravaged fields, hunger.

Laurélien Laurore held out his hand to Manuel. "I'm going to leave, brother. Take a rest after your long journey. I'd like to chat with you some other time about that country of Cuba. So I say, *adieu, oui.*"

"*Adieu*, friend."

One after the other, they shook hands with him, and left the house repeating, "Délira, cousin, *adieu, oui.* Bienaimé, brother, *adieu, oui.*"

"*Adieu*, neighbors," the old folks responded, "and thanks for your kindness."

From his doorstep, Manuel watched them disappear along various paths through the woods toward their huts.

"You must be hungry," his mother said. "I'm going to fix you something to eat. There isn't much, you know."

Under the shed of palm leaves she squatted before three blackened rocks, lighted the fire and patiently nursed the newborn flame, fanning it with the palm of her hand.

She thought ecstatically, There's a light on his forehead!

The sun sank in the sky. It wouldn't be long before the Angelus sounded; still a mist of heat thickened by dust clung to the rim of the thorn acacias.

Chapter Three

IT MUST BE ALMOST DAY, Manuel mused. Under the door crept the dull light of dawn, with its slight freshness. He heard aggressive roosters crowing in the yard, the beating of wings and the busy scratching of the chickens. He opened the door. The sky was turning pale in the east, but the woods still reposed in a mass of shadow.

The little dog greeted him ill humoredly, bared his fangs peevishly, and wouldn't stop growling.

"There's a hateful dog for you, a dog that don't like anybody," old Délira exclaimed. She was already busy heating the coffee. "You're up early, son. Did you have a good sleep?"

"*Bonjour, mama.* Papa, I bid you *bonjour, oui.*"

"How goes it, son?" Bienaimé replied. He dipped a bit of cassava in his coffee. Délira offered Manuel a small mug of fresh water. He washed his mouth and his eyes.

"I didn't sleep," Bienaimé complained, "no, I didn't sleep well. I woke up in the middle of the night, and kept turning over and over till morning."

"Maybe it was happiness itching you," Délira observed with a smile.

"What happiness?" the old man retorted. "It was more than likely fleas."

While Manuel was drinking his coffee, a red glow ascended, spreading above the mountains. The savanna and its kinky bushes grew spacious in the light and stretched to the frontier where dawn disengaged itself from the dark embrace of night. In the woods, the wild guinea fowl uttered their vehement call.

Anyhow, it's good soil, Manuel was thinking. The mountains are ruined, that's true, but the plain can still produce its full measure of corn, millet, and all kinds of crops. What it needs is irrigation.

As in a dream, he saw the water running through the canals like a network of veins transporting life to the depths of the soil—banana trees swaying under the silky caress of the wind, ears beaded with corn, plots of sweet potatoes strewn over the fields, all this burnt earth changed into verdant colors. He turned to his father. "And Fanchon Spring?"

"What about Fanchon Spring?" Bienaimé was filling his pipe with what was left of yesterday's cigar stump.

"What about its water?"

"Dry as the palm of my hand."

"And Lauriers Spring?"

"You're a persistent Negro! Not a drop there either. All that's left is Zombi Pool, but that's a pond of mosquitoes, water as rotten as a dead adder, thick stagnant water too weak to flow."

Manuel remained silent; a stubborn pucker contracted his lips. Bienaimé dragged his chair toward the calabash tree, and sat down, leaning back against the trunk. He faced the road, where the peasant women were passing, leading their panting beasts of burden.

"Get up, burro, get along!" Their shrill voices rose in the morning stillness.

"Mama, how are you going to keep alive?"

"By the grace of God," Délira murmured. She added sadly, "But there isn't any mercy for the poor."

"Resignation won't get us anywhere." Manuel shook his head impatiently. "Resignation is treacherous. It's just the same as discouragement. It breaks your arms. You keep on expecting miracles and providence, with your rosary in your hand, without doing a thing. You pray for rain, you pray for a harvest, you recite the prayers of the saints and the *loas*. But providence—take my word for it—is a man's determination not to accept misfortune, to overcome the earth's bad will every day, to bend the whims of the water to your needs. Then the earth will call you, 'Dear Master.' The water will call you, 'Dear Master.' And there's no providence but hard work, no miracles but the fruit of your hands."

Délira looked at him with an anxious tenderness. "You have a clever tongue, and you've traveled to foreign lands. You've learned things that pass my understanding. I'm just a poor old stupid black woman. Still, you don't give the Good Lord his due. He is the Lord of all things! In his hands he holds the changing of the seasons, the thread of the rain, and the life of his creatures. He gives radiance to the sun and lights the candles of the stars. He blows on the day and changes it to night. He controls the spirits of the springs, the sea, and of the trees. 'Papa Loko,' he says, 'Master Agoué,' he says, 'do you hear me?' Loko-atisou answers, 'Thy will be done.' And Agoueta-woyo answers, 'Amen.' Have you forgotten these things?"

"I haven't heard them for a long time, mama."

Manuel was smiling. Délira, somewhat abashed, sighed, "Ah! my son, it's the truth, *oui*."

Now it was broad daylight. The sun set fire to the summits of the hills. The erosion stood out in the raw light. The fields appeared in all their nakedness. On the savanna the oxen, exasperated by the ticks, bellowed deeply. The smoke from the charcoal burners' fires floated above the thorn acacias. Manuel went to get his machete.

"I'm going to walk around a bit, mama."

"Where?"

"Over that way." He made a vague gesture toward the mountains.

"I'll be waiting for you. Don't dally on the road too long, son."

Seeing him walk off toward the woods, Bienaimé grumbled, "He's no sooner got here than he begins to wander off."

Manuel traversed the still-darkened woods whose branches touched the cactus-hemmed path. He remembered that after the detours and crossings, the road would open on a narrow valley where Bienaimé formerly had cleared a patch of cotton land. Then, through a notch in the mountain, it would lead to the spring.

He startled a flock of guinea hens that flew noisily away across a thicket of logwood. "I would try to trap one, but guineas are smarter than doves or ortolans." He was full of happiness despite the stubborn thoughts that haunted him. He wanted to sing a greeting to the trees: "Growing things, my growing things! To you I say, 'Honor!' You must answer 'Respect,' so that I may enter. You're my house, you're my country. Growing things, I say, vines of my woods, I am planted in this soil. I am rooted in this earth. To all that grows, I say, 'Honor.' Answer 'Respect,' so that I may enter."

He proceeded at that long, almost nonchalant but graceful gait of a Negro of the plain, sometimes cutting a path with a swift stroke of his machete. He was still humming when he reached a clearing. A peasant was building up a charcoal pit. He was black, thick-set and as short as if he had been hammered down by a rammer. His enormous hands dangled at the ends of his arms like bundles of roots. His hair grew low on his stubborn brow, thin and kinky.

Manuel greeted him, but the man merely looked at him without answering. Under protruding eyebrows, his glance shifted like that of a distrustful animal in a bushy hole. Finally he said, "Are you the Negro who returned from Cuba yesterday?"

"I am."

"You're Bienaimé's son?"

"I am."

His glance narrowed to become no more than a burning cinder. The peasant looked Manuel up and down, then with calculated slowness he turned his head, spat, and returned to his charcoal pit.

Manuel struggled between surprise and anger. One second more of this red veil over his eyes, and he would have repaid the stranger's insolence with the flat of his machete across his cranium, but he controlled himself.

He continued his walk, ruminating over his indignation and his uneasiness. "That son of a bitch!" he muttered in Spanish. "But what's behind it?" He remembered the sudden change in Annaise's attitude. "There's something strange in all that!"

The valley lay at the foot of the mountain. The waters, dashing down from the heights, had hollowed it out and the soil, washed away, had drifted down the slope to be lost in the distance. Bones of rocks pierced its thin layer of skin, and now spider plants covered with prickles had overrun it.

Manuel went up the mountainside under the glare of the sun. Once he glanced toward the sickly-colored plain, the grayish foliage of the thorn acacias, the ravine unfolding its long pebbled gully to the sun. He turned down a path which descended obliquely toward the ravine where formerly had gushed Fanchon Spring.

Slabs of stone polished by water sounded under his feet. He had known them covered by humid moss. He recalled the pure water, its long ripple without beginning or end, and the breath of the wind like wet clothes torn by the gusts of air. The spring came from far away, Manuel thought. It came from the very kidneys of the mountain, winding secretly, patiently filtering through the dark to appear at last in the mountain gap, free of mud, fresh, clear, and innocent as a blind man's glance.

Now only a seam of gravel and couch grass remained, and, farther on, where the flat of the valley began, blocks of rock, having rolled down the mountain, were resting like peaceful cattle around a big thorny *sablier* tree.

He had wanted to see for himself. Well, he knew now. The same was probably true of Lauriers Spring—a hole of caked mud and that was all. So he would have to resign himself to slow death, to sink irremediably in the quicksands of poverty, and say to the soil, "*Adieu*, I give up!"

No! Behind the mountains there were other mountains, and may the lightning strike him dead if he didn't dig through the veins in their ravines with his own fingernails until he found water, until he felt its wet tongue on his hand!

"Old man, you haven't see a red mare around here, have you? It was Laurélien's voice. "The rascal has broken her rope." Awkwardly, he descended the slope toward Manuel. "So you're getting to know the country once again, brother?"

"Hearing and seeing are two different things," Manuel replied. "That's why I came here early this morning. I was saying in my mind, I was saying to myself, 'Maybe a little hidden streamlet remains.' Sometimes it happens that water gets lost in a strainer of sand, then it drips and drips until it hits hard rock and eats its way out through the earth."

With his machete he detached a brittle clod, broke it on a stone. It was full of dead twigs and the residue of dried roots that he crushed in his fingers.

"Look, there isn't anything left. The water has dried up in the very entrails of the mountain. It's not worthwhile looking any farther. It's useless." Then, with sudden anger, "But why, damn it! did you cut the woods down, the oaks, the mahogany trees, and everything else that grew up there? Stupid people with no sense!"

Laurélien struggled for a moment to find words. "What else could we do, brother? We cleared it to get new wood. We cut it down for framework and beams for our huts. We repaired the fences around our fields. We didn't know, ourselves. Ignorance and need go together, don't they?"

The sun scratched the scorched back of the mountain with its shining fingernails. Along the dry ravine the earth panted. The countryside, baked in drought, began to sizzle.

"It's getting late," Laurélien said. "My mare's running loose around here. She's in heat, and I'm afraid the dirty hussy will get herself covered by that bandy-legged chestnut colt of Brother Dorismond's."

Together they went up the slope. "Are you coming to the cockfight tomorrow, if-it-be-God's-will?"

"If I feel like it," said Manuel.

He had only one thing on his mind, and it made him irritable. Laurélien felt it vaguely and kept silent. Having reached the spot where the path forked up and down, Manuel stopped.

"Laurélien," he said, "I'm going to talk frankly to you. Listen to me, please. Listen carefully: This water problem is life or death for us. I spent part of the night wide awake. I was sleepless and restless because I kept thinking. Manuel, I reasoned, what's the way out of this misery? The more I thought it over, the more I realized there was only one road and a straight one at that—we've got to look for water. Every man has his own convictions, heh? Well, I swear I'll find water and I'll bring it to the plain with the rope of a canal around its neck. I'm telling you, I, Manuel Jean-Joseph!"

Laurélien stared at him in wide-eyed amazement "And how're you going to do it?"

"Wait and you'll see. But, now, just believe me and let it be a secret between us."

"May the Holy Virgin blind my eyes if I say a word!"

"Good! Then if I need your help, I can count on you?"

"Be sure of it!" Laurélien solemnly swore. They shook hands.

"Agreed?" Manuel asked.

"Agreed!"

"In truth?"

"In truth, three times."

While Manuel was going down the mountainside, Laurélien called him again. "Brother Manuel, ho!"

"What is it, *oui*, Brother Laurelien?"

"You can bet on my rooster tomorrow. There's none any braver."

Manuel skirted the thicket. The old clearing had eaten away its edges, but now a stubborn growth of arborescent cactus bristling with needles, their broad, hairy leaves thick and shiny like the skin of crocodiles, was reclaiming its rights.

When he got home, the sky, turned iron-gray, was pressing down like a hot kettle-top on the clearing in the trees. Their hut, leaning against the arbor, seemed as though abandoned for a long time. Bienaimé was nodding under the calabash tree. Life had been thrown off stride, congealed in its course. Squalls of dust swept the fields. Beyond the savanna, the horizon cut off the sight of hope.

Mending a dress that had been worn out a thousand times, worried old Délira went over the same everyday thoughts: food was getting low; they were already reduced to a few handfuls of millet and Congo beans; oh! Virgin Mary! it wasn't her fault, she had done her duty and taken precautions in keeping with the wisdom of her ancestral gods. Before sowing the corn at dawn in the vigilant red eye of the sun, she had said to the Lord Jesus Christ, turning to the east, and to the angels of Guinea, turning to the south, to the spirits of the dead, turning to the west, to the saints, turning to the north, she had said to them, as she scattered the grain in the four sacred directions:

"Jesus Christ, angels, spirits of the dead, saints, here's the corn that I give you. Give me in return the strength to work and the pleasure of reaping. Protect me from disease, and all my family, too—Bienaimé, my husband, and my boy in foreign lands. Protect this field against drought and voracious beasts. It's a favor that I ask you, if you please, through the Virgin of Miracles. Amen! And thank you!"

She raised her tired eyes to Manuel. "So you're back, my son."

"I've something to ask you, mama. But first I'm going to wash."

He took some water from the jar and filled a wooden basin. Stripped to the waist behind the hut, his skin, vigorously rubbed, took on a lustrous shine and his muscles stretched as flexibly as vines filled with sap. He returned refreshed and drew up a bench under the arbor. His mother sat near him. He related his strange adventure in the woods.

"Tell me what this Negro looks like," asked Bienaimé, who had awakened.

"He's a black man, strong and hard, with hair like grains of pepper."

"And very deep-set eyes?"

"Yes."

"That's Gervilen," Bienaimé declared. "That wretch, that dog, that vagabond!"

"And yesterday I was strolling along with a girl. We were talking in a friend-like way. But when I told her who I was, she turned her back on me."

"What was she like?" the old man inquired.

"Nice build, with large eyes, white teeth, fine skin. She told me her name—Annaise, they call her."

"That's Rosanna's daughter and Beaubrun's who's dead. Long and tall as a tree pole, and good for catching suckers! She's got eyes like a milch cow. As for her skin, I wouldn't give a damn about it! And as far as her teeth are concerned, me, I've never laughed with her enough to notice them!" Bienaimé was boiling angry and the words got all mixed up in the tufts of his beard.

"Why are we enemies?" Manuel asked.

Without answering, Bienaimé went back to his chair. Under the arbor there was a streak of shade that came from the foliage of an overhanging palm tree.

"It's an old story," the old man began. "But it hasn't been forgotten. You were in Cuba at the time." He munched on his pipestem. "Blood was shed."

"Tell me about it, papa. I'm listening," Manuel said politely.

"Well, son, when the late Johannes Longeannis died— we called him General Longeannis because he had fought with the Cacos—we had to divide up the land. He was really a rich peasant, if you remember, that General Longeannis, a well-mannered Negro, a patriarch. They don't come like that anymore. Through him, we were all related, more or less. He had so many children you can't count them. My own great-aunt bore him Dorisca, Gervilen's father—may the curse of hell fall on his scaly head! Dividing up property gives you plenty of arguments, it's true, but it's all in the family, isn't it? And folks finally get it straightened out. One says, 'Do you understand, Brother So-and-So?' And Brother So-and-So replies, 'I understand.' And each takes his piece of land. The soil isn't a piece of cloth. There's room for everybody.

"But Dorisca was as deaf as a stubborn mule, and one fine day he comes along with his family and a bunch of supporters and takes possession. The rest of us—well, you'll see what happened. At that time they were in the very middle of the *coumbite*, Dorisca and his gang, and they hadn't been going slow on white rum. My brother; poor dead Sauveur Jean-Joseph—may God have pity on his soul!—not being a coward, approached first."

" 'Brother Dorisca,' he said, 'you aren't within your rights.' And Dorisca answers him, 'Get off my land, or I'll hack you in pieces that even the dogs will vomit up!' 'So you insult me!' says Sauveur. 'Excrement!' Dorisca answers, 'and your mama this and your mama that!' 'You shouldn't have said that,' Sauveur remarks, and he draws his machete more quickly than the other and stretches him out stone dead."

"Then the fight began. There were plenty of wounded. I, myself—" Bienaimé raised his jacket and ran his finger along a scar under the white hair of his chest. "Sauveur died in prison. He was my kid brother and a good man." Bienaimé wiped a tear away with his clenched fist.

"I'm listening," Manuel said.

"We finally got the land divided up, with the help of the justice of the peace. But we also divided up all that hate between us. Before, we were just one big family. That's finished now. Each one nurses his own grudge and whets his own anger. There's our side—and the others. Between the two, blood! You can wade in blood!"

"That Gervilen is a man full of evil," Délira murmured. "And when he drinks, the *clairin* drives him out of his head."

"He's a Negro with no conscience," Bienaimé amended.

Head down, Manuel listened. Thus a new enemy had come into being in the village and had divided it as surely as a boundary line. It was hate with its bitter brooding over the bloody past, its fratricidal quarrels.

"What's that you're saying?" Bienaimé asked.

Manuel stood up. He could see the thatched roofs through the trees, and in each hut the black poison of vengeance brewed. "I say it's a pity."

"I don't understand you, son."

But Manuel had started slowly toward the fields. He was walking in the sunlight. He was trampling on the withered plants, and his back was bent a little as though he were carrying a heavy load.

Chapter Four

A FEW DAYS LATER, Manuel was repairing the arbor. He was replacing a worm-eaten crossbar with a young logwood trunk. He had lopped off its branches, stripped its bark, and set it out to dry. But the wood still sweated a bit of reddish moisture.

"It's a good thing you're fixing the arbor," his mother said.

"It was all decayed," Manuel replied absent-mindedly.

His mother waited a while. "Because I've notified Dorméus."

"Dorméus?"

"The *houngan*, son." Manuel tested the crossbar. "Did you hear me, little one?"

"I heard you, *oui*." He was driving nails in the tender flesh of the logwood.

"It'll be day after tomorrow, if-God-wills," said Délira.

"If-God-wills," Manuel repeated.

"Bienaimé's gone to get fresh leaves to cover the arbor. It's a solemn duty that we have to carry out."

Manuel stepped down from the bench. He had finished.

"It's he, Papa Legba, who showed you the way home. Clairemise saw him in her dream, Atibon-Legba, Master of the Crossroads. We must thank him. I've already invited the family and the neighbors. Tomorrow you'll go to town to buy five gallons of white rum and two bottles of brown rum."

"I'll go," Manuel agreed.

Two evenings later, the peasants were waiting under the freshly decorated arbor. Candles stuck on the posts were burning with an acrid odor and, as the breeze flapped its wings, they would lick the darkness with smoky tongues.

The sound of voices on the road announced Dorméus' arrival. Bienaimé was already awaiting him at the gate. The *houngan* advanced; he was a tall, reddish Negro, grave in each of his movements. Many of his women helpers, his *hounsi*, in headcloths and robes of immaculate white, followed him, and they were holding lighted pine knots high in their hands. They preceded La Place, in charge of the ceremonial, the standard-bearers, the drum-and-cymbal-players.

Bowing, Bienaimé offered Dorméus a pitcher of water. The *houngan* accepted it gravely, and, with both hands, slowly lifted it toward the four cardinal points. His lips were muttering secret words. Then he sprinkled the soil, traced a magic circle, drew himself up to his full height, and began to sing, accompanied by all his aides:

> *Papa Legba, open the gate for us! Ago, ye!*
> *Atibon Legba! Oh! open the gate for us,*
> *So that we may pass!*
> *We'll thank the great gods, loa yo!*
> *Papa Legba, master of the three crossroads!*
> *Master of the three canals!*
> *Open the gate for us!*
> *Let us in!*
> *When we get in,*
> *We'll thank the loa yo!*

"Come in, papa, come in," said Bienaimé, humbly giving way before the *houngan*.

Dorméus took the lead, followed by his helpers. The torches cast a furtive light on the *hounsi's* white robes and struck a few sparks of gilded spangles from the banners. The others advanced in a mass darker than the night.

And Legba, that old god of Guinea, was there. Under the arbor, he had just taken on the form of Fleurimond, but had changed him into his own venerable image in keeping with his ageless age. His shoulders bent and his body panting with fatigue, he leaned on the improvised crutch of a twisted branch.

The peasants opened a "path of respect" for the *houngan*. Over the possessed, the standard-bearers waved a canopy of unfurled banners. Dorméus drew the magic circle at his feet, and planted a lighted candle in the middle.

"Your children salute you," he said to Legba. "They offer you this service in gratitude and thanksgiving." He pointed to a straw sack that hung from the center post "Here's your bag with the food you'll need for your return trip. Nothing is missing. There's an ear of roasted corn soaked in syrup and olive oil, salt fish, cakes, and liquor for your thirst."

"Thank you," said the *loa* in a scarcely audible voice, "thank you for the food and drink. I see that your affairs are going badly with this drought. But that will change, that will pass. The good and the bad make a cross. I, Legba, I'm the master of this crossroad. I'll help my Creole children find the right road. They will leave behind this road of misery."

A chorus of entreaties encircled him. "Do that for us, papa, we beg you! Ah! dear papa, if you please! This penance is too much to bear! Without you we're helpless! Forgive us, forgive us! Have mercy!"

The possessed acquiesced with a senile nod. His hand trembled on his crutch, and he again uttered a few breathless, unintelligible words. Dorméus gave a signal. The drums beat a jerky introduction, then grew into a deep rhythmic volume that burst upon the night. A unanimous chant arose, based on ancient rhythms, and the peasants began to dance their supplication, knees bent, arms outstretched:

> *Legba, show us how!*
> *Alegba-sé, it's you and me!*

Dancing this same *Yanvalou*, their fathers had implored the fetishes of Whydah. Now in these days of distress, they remembered it with a fidelity that brought back from the night of time the dark powers of the old Dahomey gods:

> *It's you and me, Kataroulo,*
> *Mighty Legba, it's you and me!*

The *hounsi*, circling around the central pole, mingled the foam of their white robes with the rolling hips of the peasants dressed in blue. Délira, too, was dancing, with a meditative expression on her face. And Manuel, conquered by the magic beat of the drums in the depths of his being, was dancing and singing with the rest.

> *Cry glory, Atibon Legba!*
> *Glory, Kataroulo!*
> *Mighty Legba!*

Dormeus shook his *asson*, the ritual rattle made of a hollow gourd, adorned by a trellis of adder's vertebrae intertwined with glass pearls. The drums quieted down. In the center of the magic circle, on a white napkin, La Place had set a rooster the color of flame, so as to concentrate in one living entity, in a burning bush of feathers and blood, all natural forces. Dormeus seized the rooster and waved it like a fan above those offering the sacrifice.

Mérila and Clairemise staggered, trembling, their faces distorted. They were dancing now, and their shoulders struggled in the passionate grip of the *loa* who possessed them in flesh and spirit.

"*Santa Maria Gratia!*"

The peasants began to sing the chant of thanksgiving, for this was the visible sign that Legba accepted their sacrifice. With a violent twist, Dormeus snatched off the cock's head and presented its body to the four cardinal points of the compass.

"*Abobo!*" the *hounsi* screamed.

The *houngan* repeated the same gesture of orientation and let three drops of blood fall to the ground.

"Blood! ... Blood! ... Blood!" the peasants chanted.

Délira knelt at Bienaimé's side all the while, her palms together before her face. She looked for Manuel, but he was inside the hut drinking a glass of *clairin* with Laurélien and Lhérisson Célhomme.

"Ah! We must serve the old gods of Guinea, *oui*," Laurélien was saying.

"Our life is in their hands," Lhérisson replied.

Manuel emptied his glass. The harsh hammering of the drums sustained the exaltation of the chant. "Let's go see what's happening," he suggested.

Blood was dripping from the cock, widening a crimson circle on the ground. The *houngan*, the *hounsi*, Délira and Bienaimé dipped a finger in it and made the sign of the cross on their foreheads.

"I've been looking all over for you," said the old woman in a tone of reproach.

He hardly heard her. Like a frenzied tornado, the *hounsi* were dancing and singing around the fowl of the sacrifice. As they passed, they tore out its feathers by the handful until they had plucked it clean.

Antoine received the victim from the *houngan's* hands. Antoine was no longer the hilarious Simidor, bristling with gossip like a cactus with prickles. Ceremonious and conscious of his importance, he now represented Legba-of-the-Old-Bones, entrusted with cooking, without garlic or lard, what was no longer an ordinary cock, but the *Koklo* of the gods, endowed with this ritual name and the sanctity that his sacred death conferred upon him.

"Be careful, brother," he said to a peasant who bumped into him.

He immediately became silent, terrified. For it wasn't Duperval Jean-Louis, this man who was wildly jumping up and down with face convulsed. It was Ogoun, the fearful *loa*, god of the blacksmiths and god of killers. And he was screaming in a thunderous voice:

"It's me, it's me, it's me! Negro Olicha Baguita Wanguita!"

Dorméus came over to him brandishing his rattle. Trembling all over, the possessed man brayed, "It's me, it's me, it's me! Negro Batala! Negro Ashade Boko!"

In the *houngan's* hands the rattle sounded with dry authority. "Papa Ogoun," said Dorméus, "don't be difficult. I beg your pardon, but this service isn't for you. Days come, days go—next time it will be your turn. Let us continue this ceremony." The possessed man was frothing, reeling violently right and left, driving back the circle of peasants surrounding him.

"Don't insist," Dorméus continued, but with less assurance since there was nothing he could do about it. Ogoun became stubborn, he wouldn't go, he demanded his share of the honor. La Place presented him his saber which he kissed, and the *hounsi* tied a red madras about his head, attached others about his arms, and Dorméus marked out a magic circle on the ground to permit the god to make his entrance. They brought him a chair and he sat down, a bottle of rum and he drank in long swallows, a cigar and he began to smoke.

"So," he said, "this fellow Manuel has returned! Where is Manuel?"

"Here I am, *oui*," said Manuel.

"Answer me, '*Oui*, papa.'"

"*Oui*, papa."

"One would say that you're impertinent, isn't that so?"

"No."

"Answer me, 'No, papa!'"

"No, papa."

The possessed man bounded to his feet, roughly pushed back the *hounsi*, and began to dance and sing:

> *Bolada Kimalada! O Kimalada!*
> *We'll dig the canal! Ago!*
> *We'll dig a canal, I say! Ago yé!*
> *The vein is open, the blood flows.*
> *The vein is open, the blood flows! Ho!*
> *Bolada Kimalada! O Kimalada!*

He swayed backward and forward in a Nago dance, alone in the midst of the frightened peasants, then he slowed down to little jumps. Still puffing, still trembling, but more feebly for the *loa* was departing, the stupid face of Duperval slowly reappeared beneath the warlike mask of Ogoun. A few more uncertain steps, a few more spasmodic twists of the head, and Duperval crumpled, the *loa* had departed. With the aid of Dieuveille Riché, Manuel lifted the man and carried him to one side. He was as heavy and lifeless as the trunk of a tree.

"Bienaimé," Délira whispered, "Bienaimé, my man, I don't like what Papa Ogoun sang, no. My heart is heavy. I don't know what's come over me."

But Dorméus continued the Legba service with the ceremony of the *asogwe*. Bienaimé, Délira, and Manuel took the straw bag in their hands together and presented it successively to the four cardinal points. The *houngan* planted the cock feathers about the pole, traced a new magic circle and lighted a candle at its center. The banners waved, the dull rumble of the drum resounded, urging the chant on to a new outburst. The women's voices shot up very high, cracking the thick mass of song:

Legba-sé! Legba!
Blood has been drawn!
Blood! Abobo!
Mighty Legba!
Seven Legba Kataroulos!
Mighty Legba!
Alegba-sé!
You and me!
Ago yé!

Manuel let himself go in the upsurge of the dance, but a strange sadness crept into his soul. He caught his mother's eye and thought he saw tears shining there.

Now the sacrifice to Legba was over. The Master of the Roads had gone back to his native Guinea by that mysterious path which *loas* tread.

Nevertheless, the fête went on. The peasants forgot their troubles. Dancing and drinking anesthetized them—swept away their shipwrecked souls to drown in those regions of unreality and danger where the fierce forces of the African gods lay in wait.

When dawn came over the sleepless plain, the drums were still beating like a heart that never tires.

Chapter Five

LIFE BEGAN AGAIN, but it didn't change. It followed the same routine, the same beaten path, with cruel indifference. They were up before dawn. Through the cracks in the obscure sky, the first confused gleams of light passed and scattered. Later, the silhouette of the hill became visible, fringed in pale limpidity.

As soon as the sun touched the woods enough to light its intersecting paths through the thorn acacias, Manuel would be off. He would fell some trees, and in the clearing he would set up his charcoal pit beneath which the wood was to burn in a slow fire. Then he would walk toward the mountains. He'd return from his promenade bathed in perspiration, his hands covered with earth. Délira would ask where he had been. He'd answer evasively, with that stubborn pucker at the corner of his mouth.

Every Saturday, Délira would load two burros with charcoal and go to the city. She would return at nightfall with a few wretched provisions and a bit of change. Then she'd sit in her hut broken down under the weight of an immense fatigue. Bienaimé would demand his tobacco and would never find it strong enough.

At times the old woman related the vexations she encountered. The market inspectors, posted at the gates of the city, would pounce on the peasant women and fleece them mercilessly.

"He comes up and asks me to pay. I show him that I've already paid. He gets angry and begins to swear. 'Look, if you're not ashamed,' I say to him, 'look at my white hair. How would you like your own mother to be treated like this?' 'Shut your trap!' he yells, that's what he yells, 'or else I'll drag you to jail for rebellion and public scandal.' I had to give him the money. No, they don't have any consideration for us poor folks."

Manuel clenched his fists hard enough to make them crack.

"Bandit! No-good Negro!" Bienaimé growled. A moment later he said, "Go to bed, my poor old woman. You can't hold your eyes open. You've covered a lot of ground."

Délira unrolled her mat and spread it on the dirt. Despite Manuel's protests, she had insisted on his occupying the mahogany bed in the other room.

Sometimes Antoine would come by during the day. He would squat down near Bienaimé.

"Ah! song-leader, Simidor," the old man would say, "have you ever seen such misery?"

The Simidor would shake his head. "Never before." And gazing sadly at the charred fields, he would add in a subdued tone, "Don't call me Simidor. Call me Antoine. That's my name. You see, brother, when you say 'Simidor,' that makes me think of the good old days. It's bitter to remember, it's bitter as gall."

On the porch in the afternoons Manuel wove hats of macaw straw. They would easily sell for six cents apiece in the next town. The vodun ceremony had eaten up what little money he had brought from Cuba. Dorméus alone had cost eight dollars.

Often Laurélien came to see him. He'd sit on the bench. His large, twisted hands, made for wielding the hoe, rested on his knees. Softly he'd ask, "What about the water?"

"Not yet, not yet," Manuel would reply. "But I'm on its trail."

His nimble fingers would be moving up and down while his thoughts traveled toward Annaise. Several times he had seen her in the village. Each time she'd turned away. She had walked off with that long, nonchalant, swinging step of hers.

Laurélien would ask once again, "Tell me about Cuba."

"It's a country five times, no, ten, no, perhaps twenty times as large as Haiti. But, you know, I'm made out of this, I am." He touched the earth, caressing its soil. "That's what I am, this very earth! I've got it in my blood. Look at my color. Folks could say the soil has faded on me, and on you, too. This land is the black man's. Each time they've tried to take it from us, we have cleaned out injustice with the blades of our machetes."

"Yes, but in Cuba there's more wealth. Folks live more at ease. Here, we've got to struggle hard with life, and what does it get us? We don't even have enough to fill our bellies, and we've no rights at all against the crookedness of the authorities. The justice of the peace, the rural police, the surveyors, the food speculators live on us like fleas. I spent a month in prison with a bunch of thieves and assassins, just because I went in town without shoes. And where could I have gotten the money to buy them, I ask you, brother? What are we, us peasants? Barefooted Negroes, scorned and mistreated."

"What are we? Since that's your question, I'm going to answer you. We're *this country*, and it wouldn't be a thing without us, nothing at all. Who does the planting? Who does the watering? Who does the harvesting? Coffee, cotton, rice, sugar cane, cacao, corn, bananas, vegetables, and all the fruits, who's going to grow them if we don't? Yet with all that, we're poor, that's true. We're out of luck, that's true. We're miserable, that's true. But do you know why, brother? Because of our ignorance. We don't know yet what a force we are, what a single force—all the peasants, all the Negroes of plain and hill, all united. Some day, when we get wise to that, we'll rise up from one end of the country to the other. Then we'll call a General Assembly of the Masters of the Dew, a great big *coumbite* of farmers, and we'll clear out poverty and plant a new life."

"You're talking sense, *oui*," Laurélien said.

He had almost lost his breath trying to follow Manuel. A wrinkle on his brow marked the effort of his meditation. In the most inarticulate corner of his brain, accustomed to slowness and patience, a curtain of light began to rise. It illumined a sudden hope, still obscure and distant, but as certain as brotherhood. He spat a jet of saliva through his teeth.

"What you're saying is as clear as water running in the sunlight." He was standing, and his hands were contracting as if to try to hold on to fugitive words.

"You're going already?"

"Yes, I was just passing by before I went to see about the cattle. I'll think over your words. They've got plenty of weight. You can be sure of that, *oui*. So, goodbye, Chief."

"Why do you call me, 'Chief?' " Manuel asked, astonished.

Laurélien lowered his head, reflected. "I don't know why, myself," he said.

He walked away at his peaceful solid gait. Manuel followed him with his eyes until he disappeared among the trees.

A compact, blinding light inflamed the surface of sky and earth. The plaintive cooing of a dove was heard. One couldn't tell where it was coming from. It rolled on the breast of silence with depressing notes. The wind had died down. The fields lay flat under the weight of the sun, with their thirsty soil, their blighted plants. On a distant mound, overlooking the confused expanse of thorn acacias, the leaves of the macaw trees drooped inert as broken wings.

Before each hut, in the shade of the few trees that the drought had spared, peasants brooded over their ill fortune. Quarrels exploded without any apparent motive. The chattering of the women became irritable, turned easily into argument. The youngsters kept out of reach of cuffs, but their prudence did them no good. One would hear an angry voice shout:

"Philogène? Oh! Missieu Philogène, don't you hear me calling you? " And Philogène would draw near, with death in his soul, to receive a resounding smack on the back of his head.

In fact, things had grown even worse. Hunger was really making itself felt. The price of blue denim was getting higher in the city. It was useless to mend clothes. There were folks whose hind parts (begging your pardon) appeared through holes in their trousers like the crescents of a black moon in the cleft of a cloud—which wasn't at all respectable. No, you couldn't even pretend that it was.

On Sunday at the cockfight, white rum flavored with cinnamon bark, lemon or anis, quickly went to the peasants' heads, especially those of the losers. And there were times when clubs were called into play. Thank heaven, it didn't go any further, not so far as the machete, fortunately, and a few days later the opponents would become reconciled. But one couldn't be sure that they wouldn't nurse a bit of left-over spite deep inside themselves.

"Manuel," said Bienaimé, "suppose you go and see where the white-spotted calf has wandered off to, suppose you go and see?" Manuel stopped his work, untied the rope that was hanging on a nail, and tested it to see how strong it was. "Tie her to a pole, but give her plenty of rope so she won't get tangled up."

"Why don't you wait till she's bigger?" Délira asked. "Till she gives birth to a calf that we can sell later on in her stead?"

"And what'll we live on in the meantime? By then we'll eat our own teeth down to the gums," the old man retorted.

Since the fenced-in fields bordered it on one side and the woods on the other, the savanna served as an enclosure for the cattle. The peasants got a bit of milk of poor quality from the cows. But, ordinarily, the animals lived in wild freedom and were captured only to be branded with a red-hot iron, or to be sold at the Pont Beudet market when there was an urgent need for a little currency.

A kind of short, dry weed grew in little patches like wild hair on warts, and, except under the umbrella of a rare logwood tree, the sun exercised its limitless domination.

"With irrigation it could be rich with Guinea grass," Manuel mused.

He saw the heifer. She stood out in the savanna with her coat spotted in red and white. He cut in, to catch her as quickly as possible by blocking off all retreat and pushing her against the circle of chandelier cactus that lined Saint-Julien's field. She detected the maneuver and began to run toward open country. With long strides, Manuel raced after her, and lassoed her on the run. She dragged him along, but he pulled firmly, jerking on the rope, pacifying her imperiously with his voice. "Whoa, frisky lady! Whoa, you brigand! Whoa, pretty cow, whoa!"

He succeeded in casting the end of the rope about a stump. The heifer struggled, butting in all directions, but in the end she had to admit defeat. Manuel waited for a moment, then led her toward a logwood tree and tied her in the shade.

"You're going to change masters," he said, patting her snout. "You're going to leave the big savanna. That's how life is, after all." The heifer looked at him with wide sorrowful eyes, and bleated. Manuel patted her back and her sides with the palm of his hand. "You're not any too fat," he said. "To feel your bones, just touch you. You won't bring a good price. No, you surely won't."

The sun was now sliding down the slope of the sky which, under a diluted and transparent mist of clouds, was turning the color of indigo in soapy water. Behind the woods, a high flaming barrier hurled sulfur darts into the bleeding west.

Manuel returned to the main road and went through the village. The huts were laid out at random along scattered paths in the yards. Something more than trees, gardens, and hedges separated them. Anger, secret and repressed, that a spark could ignite into violence, aggravated by poverty, gave each peasant as he faced his neighbor that stitched-up mouth, that evasive glance, that hand itching for a blow. One could see that all these years the past had never been buried with Dorisca and Sauveur. They kept it ever fresh like a half-closed wound continually irritated by a fingernail.

The womenfolks were the most enraged. They were truly furious. That was because they were the first to know that there was nothing to put on the fire, that the children were crying from hunger, that they were wasting away, their limbs thin and twisted like dry branches, their stomachs enormous. Sometimes the women would go out of their heads and insult each other, on occasion, even with words that aren't allowed. But women's insults don't lead anywhere, they're just so much wind. More serious was the silence of the men.

Manuel was thinking of all that as he walked through the settlement. There were some whom he greeted. "*Adieu,* brother," he would say.

"Oh! *adieu,* Manuel," the other would answer.

"How are you?" Manuel would ask.

"We're fighting for life," the other would reply.

But some turned away as he passed, or else stared right through him as though he were smoke.

Nevertheless, he knew them well. Were they not Pierrilis, Similien, Mauléon, Ismael, Termonfils, Josaphat? He had grown up with them in these woods, had taken part in their games, had set traps for ortolans in the savanna, had stolen ears of corn by their side. Later, in the *coumbites,* their voices and their husky young strength had mingled. Ah, how they had cleared and cleaned Brother Merville's field formerly— even that day when they had drunk a bit too much white rum! Yes, he remembered it all. He had forgotten nothing.

He wanted to walk up to them and say, "Well, cousins, don't you remember me? It's I, Manuel, Manuel Jean-Joseph, himself and no other." But their faces were like dark unlighted walls.

No, there was neither justice nor sense in this business. One should let the dead rest in the peace of the cemetery under the red jasmine. They had nothing to do with the ways of the living, these ghosts that returned in broad daylight, these obstinate blood-stained phantoms. Besides, if he found water, everyone's help would be needed. It wouldn't be a small matter to bring it down to the plain. They would have to organize a great *coumbite* of all the peasants. Thus the water would bring them together again. Its cool breath would dispel the evil odor of spite and hatred. With the new plants, with the fruit- and corn-laden fields, the earth overflowing with simple fecund life, a brotherly community would be reborn. Yes, he'd go and find them, and talk with them. They had good sense, they would understand.

In front of his door, Hilarion, the rural policeman, was playing at *trois-sept* with his assistant. He squinted from his cards to Manuel.

"Hello," he said. "You're the very one I want to see. Wait a minute! I've something to tell you." And to his opponent, "Ten of diamonds! Give me your ace."

"I haven't any ace."

"Give me that ace!" Hilarion exclaimed threateningly. The assistant put down his ace. "Cheat! Sassy rascal, you!" Hilarion cried in triumph. He covered the cards in the hollow of his hand as he turned toward Manuel. "So you're going around talking with the peasants, heh?"

Manuel waited.

"You're talking all kind of talk, it seems." A flash of malevolence came into the slit of his eyes. "Well, they aren't to the liking of the authorities, they're words of rebellion." He unfolded his cards like a fan. "Don't say I didn't warn you!"

Manuel smiled. "Is that all?"

"That's all," Hilarion answered, his head in his cards.

"Ten of clubs! Nine of clubs! Give me your ace!"

"But I haven't got any ace," the other moaned in desperation.

"Give me that ace right now!" The assistant surrendered the ace of clubs. "Ah, you monkey!" shouted the hilarious Hilarion. "You thought yourself slick enough to play Hilarion Hilaire! That'll teach you, you rascal, you!"

His loud vulgar laughter resounded as Manuel walked away. He wasn't uneasy. Often he had talked to Laurélien, Saint-Julien, Riché, and the others. Surely they hadn't reported his words, but merely discussed and repeated them, and, like flies who get caught in a spider web, they had reached the hairy ears of Hilarion. It was a good sign, after all, that they were spreading.

Children were following him, fascinated by his great height. To them, he was the man who had crossed the sea, who had lived in the strange country of Cuba. He was crowned with a halo of mysteries and legends. Manuel caught one of them by the arm. He was a very black little Negro, with eyes as round and shiny as marbles. He patted the boy's head that had been shaved with the bottom of a bottle.

"What's your name?"

"Monpremier, *oui*."

But a woman's voice snapped crossly, "You, Monpremier, come here!" The youngster scampered off toward the hut. In his haste his heels hammered his bare buttocks.

Manuel went on, his heart ill at ease. He left the last huts behind him.

Golden thistles covered the ruts in the path with their tiny suns. A reflection of oblique light spread slowly across the plain, but shadows were already nestling in the trees, and mauve spots were spreading over the hillsides. What had been harsh and hostile in the light became tranquil and reconciled itself to the end of the day.

Away down the road, he saw her coming. He recognized her at once by her dark dress, her white madras, because she was tall, because only she had that clean supple stride, those gently swaying hips—and because he was waiting for her.

He walked slowly toward her. "I bid you *bonsoir, oui,* Annaise." There were a few steps between them.

"Get out of my way!" She was breathing hard, her breasts heaved.

"Tell me what I've done to you and why we're enemies."

She hid her face from him. "I don't have to explain anything to you. I'm in a hurry. Let me by."

"Answer me first. I don't mean you any harm, Annaise. I like you. Honest, I do."

She sighed, "*Ay, mes amis,* there's a stubborn man for you! You would think that he has no ears to hear with. I tell you to let me go my way, *oui.*" One could see that she was making an effort to appear impatient and displeased.

"I've looked for you all over, everywhere, but you hid as if I were the werewolf himself. I wanted to talk to you, because I know you can help me."

"*I* help *you*? How so?" she asked in surprise.

For the first time, she looked at him, and Manuel saw that there was no anger in her eyes, but only a deep sadness.

"I'll tell you, if you'll listen."

"People will see us," she objected weakly.

"Nobody's going to come. And even if they did, aren't you tired, Annaise, of all the hate there is between us these days?"

"We've got trouble enough in this life, that's true. Ah! how difficult just living has become, Manuel!" She caught herself very quickly. "Let me by! Let me pass, by the grace of God!"

"So you haven't forgotten my name?"

She answered in a whisper, "Please don't torment me."

He took her hand. She tried to withdraw it, but she had no strength. "You're a hard worker, one would say."

"Yes," she said proudly, "my hands are rough."

"I've got to have a long talk with you, you know."

"We won't have time. Night is coming. Look!"

The road began to fade away and the trees were turning black, blending with the shadows. The sky held only a hesitant glimmer, fading and distant. Alone, on the far-off edge of the horizon, a red and black cloud dissolved in the vertigo of twilight

"Are you afraid of me, Annaise?"

"I don't know," she said in a troubled whisper.

"Tomorrow, late in the afternoon, when the sun is at the foot of the mountain, I'll wait for you on the rise where the macaw trees are. Will you come?"

"No, no!" Her voice was low and frightened.

"Anna," he said. He felt her hand tremble in his. "You'll come. Won't you, Anna?"

"Ah! you torment me. I feel like I've lost my good angel. Why do you torment me, Manuel?"

He saw her eyes fill with tears and, between her supplicating lips, the moist splendor of her teeth. He released her hand.

"It's night, Anna. Go in peace, go and rest, my sweetheart."

Suddenly she was no longer there. Her bare feet, departing, made no sound.

Again he said, "I'll wait for you, Anna."

Chapter Six

UNDER THE MACAW TREES, there was a semblance of coolness. A faint breath of wind glided over the leaves in a long rustling whisper, and a bit of silvery light shimmered over them with a slight shiver like that of loosened hair. On the road, the peasant women were leading their tired donkeys. They were shouting encouragement to the animals, and the weakened echo of their monotonous cries reached Manuel. He lost sight of them behind a curtain of thorn acacias, but they reappeared farther on. It was market day and they were returning home, with a long way still to go before sunset.

At that distance, he couldn't recognize them, but he knew they were women from his own village of Fonds Rouge, and also from Ravine Sèche which was deeper in the hollow of Morne Crochu, and from settlements on the plateaus of Bellevue, Mahotière, and Boucan Corail. Through the rising dust they moved in an almost uninterrupted file. Sometimes one of them would run after her animal that had strayed to one side, and would whip him back into line by dint of oaths and lashing.

Apart from the others, a girl was coming along mounted on a chestnut horse. Manuel's blood rushed to his heart with fast, burning pulsations. She stopped, looked behind her several times, then entered one of the side roads.

"She's taking the ravine trail. She'll come out by the turn at the foot of the rise."

He listened and heard the sound of hoofs on the pebbles. It was a hesitant clop-clop drowned by a faster trampling when the horse found sand underfoot. The terrain bent its stunted bushes toward the ravine.

"That's where she'll pass, between those elm trees. I'll step out so she can see me."

Now he could hear the impact and dry rebound of the rocks on the pebbles as they rolled down the slope. She turned off the narrow path. The horse was stretching his neck and breathing hard. She was wearing a flowered calico dress and a wide straw hat held in place by a chin strap.

"Get up!" she was saying, encouraging the animal with her heels. "Get up!"

Manuel left his hiding place and she saw him. She stopped and, with a quick pull on the reins, jumped down from her mount. The horse was frothing, his sides were heaving. One could see that Annaise had hurried him along despite the rocks and the ascent. She led him by the bridle and tied him to the fork of a tree.

She moved toward him with her even, agile gait. Her breasts were high and firm, and under the folds of her dress the regal motion of her legs revealed the luscious shape of her young body. She bowed to him. "I greet you, Manuel."

"I greet you, Anna."

She touched his outstretched hand with her fingertips. Under the shade of her hat, a blue silk madras bound her forehead. Silver earrings shone in her ears.

"So you came."

"I came, you see, but I shouldn't have." She lowered her head and turned her face away. "All night long I struggled. All night long I said, 'No.' But in the morning I got dressed when the cock crowed and I went to town to have an excuse for going out."

"And did you have a good sale at the market?"

"Ah, Lord, no, brother! A few measures of corn, that's all." She remained silent for a moment, then, "Manuel?"

"I'm listening, *oui*, Anna."

"I just want to tell you, I'm one woman that goes straight. No man has ever touched me. I came because I am sure you will not take advantage of me." And then, dreamily, she asked, "Why do I trust you? Why do I listen to your words?"

"Trust is almost a mystery. It can't be bought and it has no price. You can't say, 'Sell me so much and so much.' It's more like a plot between one heart and another heart. It comes naturally and sincerely, a glance maybe or the sound of a voice is enough to tell the difference between the truth and a lie. Since the first day, listen, Anna, from the first day I saw that there's nothing false about you, that everything in you is as clear and clean as a spring, like the light in your eyes."

"Don't begin with compliments. That doesn't do any good, and it isn't necessary. I, too, after our meeting on the road, I said to myself, 'He's not like the others and he has a very sincere way about him. But what words he speaks! Jesus-Mary-Joseph! He knows too much for a poor girl like me to understand.' "

"Don't begin with compliments. That doesn't do any good, and it isn't necessary."

Both of them laughed. With head thrown back, the laughter of Annaise rose full-throated, and her teeth were moist with a gleaming whiteness.

"You laugh like a turtledove," Manuel said.

"I'll fly away like one, if you continue your flattery."

His black face lighted up in a handsome smile. "Don't you want to sit down? You won't soil your dress here."

She sat next to him, leaning against the trunk of a macaw tree, her dress spread about her, and she clasped her hands around her knees.

The plain unfolded before them, surrounded by the hills. From here they could see the mingling of acacia trees, huts dispersed in the clearings, fields abandoned to the ravages of drought, and in the glare of the savanna, scattered cattle moving. Above this desolation crows on the wing hovered. Over and over they made the same circuit, perched on the cactus, and, frightened for some reason, flayed the silence with their harsh cawing.

"What's all this talk you had for me? And I'd like to know how I, Annaise, can help a man like you?"

Manuel waited a moment to answer. He was staring in front of him with that strained and distant expression.

"You see the color of the plain," he began. "It looks like straw at the mouth of a flaming furnace. The harvest has perished. There's no more hope. How are you going to live? It would be a miracle if you did live—but then it would only be to die a slow death. And what have you done to prevent it? One thing only. Cried about your misfortune to the *loas*, offered ceremonies so that they'd make the rain fall. But all that's just so much silly monkeyshines. That doesn't count! It's useless, and it's wasting time."

"Then what *does* count, Manuel? And aren't you afraid of offending our old gods of Guinea?"

"No, I respect the customs of the old folks, but the blood of a rooster or a young goat can't make the seasons change, or alter the course of the clouds and fill them with water like bladders. The other night, at the Legba ceremonies, I danced and sang to my heart's content. I'm Negro, no? And I enjoyed myself like a real Negro. When the drums beat, I feel it in the pit of my stomach. I feel an itch in my loins and an electric current in my legs, and I've got to join the dance. But that's all there is to it for me."

"Was it in that country of Cuba that you got those ideas?"

"Experience is the staff of the blind, and I learned that what counts, since you're asking me, is rebellion, and the knowledge that man is the baker of life."

"Ah! But it's life that kneads us."

"Because you're resigned like dough, that's what you are!"

"But what can we do? Aren't we helpless and with nobody to turn to when misfortune comes? It's just fate, that's all!"

"No! As long as your arms are not lopped off and you're determined to fight. What would you say, Anna, if the valley got all painted over, if on the savanna the Guinea grass grew, high as a swollen river?"

"I'd say thanks for such good fortune."

"What would you say if the corn grew in the cool fields?"

"I'd say thanks for the blessing."

"Can't you just see the clusters of millet, and those thieving blackbirds that we've got to chase away? Can't you see the ears of corn?"

She closed her eyes. "Yes, I see."

"Can't you see the banana trees bent with the weight of their bunches?"

"Yes, yes."

"Can't you see the vegetables and the ripe fruit?"

"*Oui! Oui!*"

"You see all that wealth?"

She opened her eyes. "You've made me dream! What I see is poverty."

"Yes, that's what there could be, if there were only—what, Anna?"

"Rain. Not just a little drizzle—but big, thick, lasting rain!"

"Or else irrigation, heh?"

"But Fanchon Spring is dry, and so is Lauriers Spring."

"Suppose, Anna, suppose I discovered water? Suppose I brought it to our plain?"

She looked at him in amazement. "Could you do that, Manuel?" She gazed at each of his features with extraordinary intensity, as if, slowly, he had been revealed to her, as if she were recognizing him for the first time. She said in a voice muffled by emotion, "Yes, you'll do it. You're the man who will find water. You'll be master of the springs, you'll walk through the dew in the midst of your growing things. I know you are right—and I know you are strong."

"Not I alone, Anna. All the peasants will have a part in it, and all of us will reap the benefits of the water."

She dropped her arms in a gesture of discouragement. "Alas, Manuel! Alas, brother! All day long they sharpen their teeth with threats. One detests the other. Families are feuding. Yesterday's friends are today's enemies. They have taken two corpses for their battle flags. There's blood on those corpses and the blood is not yet dry!"

"I know, Anna, but listen carefully. It will be a hard job to bring water to Fonds Rouge. We'll need everyone's help, and if there's no reconciliation it won't work out. Let me tell you. At first, in Cuba, we had no defense and no way of resistance. One person thought himself white, another was a Negro, and there were plenty of misunderstandings among us. We were scattered like grains of sand, and the bosses walked on that sand. But when we realized that we were all alike, when we got together for the *huelga* . . . "

"What does that word mean—*huelga*?"

"You call it a strike."

"I don't know what that means, either."

Manuel showed her his open hand. "Look at this single finger—how small it is, and how weak that one is, and that other one isn't any stronger, nor is this little one either, and this last one's standing all alone by itself."

He clenched his fist.

"But now is it solid enough, firm enough, united enough? You'd say yes, wouldn't you? Well, that's what a strike is: A *NO* uttered by a thousand voices speaking as one and falling on the desk of the boss with the force of a boulder. 'No, I tell you! No, and I mean no! No work, no harvest, not a blade of grass will be cut unless you pay us a fair price for our strength and the toil of our arms!'

"And the boss, what can he do? Call the police? That's right. Because the two of them are accomplices like the skin and an undershirt.

" 'Attack those bandits for me,' he orders.

"But we're not bandits, we're workers, that's what our name is—and we hold our line stubbornly. Some of us fall, but the rest hold firm in spite of hunger, police, prison. And all this time the sugar cane is waiting and rotting. The refinery is waiting with idle teeth in its grinders. The boss is waiting with his calculations of all that he expected to fill his pockets with. In the end, he is forced to compromise.

" 'After all,' he says, 'can't we talk this thing over?'

"Of course, we can talk it over. That means we've won the battle. And why? Because we've welded ourselves into one solid mass like the shoulders of a mountain, and when man's determination is as high and as hard as a mountain, there're no powers in heaven or hell that can shake it or destroy it!"

He looked afar off toward the plain, then toward the sky, towering like a cliff of light.

"You see, the greatest thing in the world is that all men are brothers, each weighs the same on the scales of poverty and injustice."

She said humbly, "And I, what's my part?"

"I'll let you know when I find water. Then you'll begin talking to the womenfolk. Women—they're the irritable sex, I don't deny that—but they're also more sensitive and they have more heart. And there are times, you know, when the heart and the mind are one and the same thing.

"You'll say, 'Cousin So-and-so, have you heard the news?'

" 'What news?' she'll ask.

" 'They say that Bienaimé's son, that Negro named Manuel, has discovered a spring. But he says that its quite a job to bring it to the plain, that it will need a general *coumbite*, and since we're feuding that isn't possible, and the spring will remain where it is without benefiting anybody.'

"And then you'll start to turn the talk around to the drought, to poverty, and how all the children are growing weak and taking sick, and that if there were only some irrigation, all that would change completely. Then if she seems to be listening to you, you'll also tell her that this Dorisca-Sauveur story has maybe outlived its time, that the interests of the living should come before the vengeance of the dead. You'll spread these words around among all the womenfolks—but be prudent and careful. Use plenty of 'It's a pity, *oui*!'—'and yet'— 'perhaps after all.' Do you understand, my *Négresse*?"

"I understand, and I'll obey you, Negro of mine."

"If it works, the womenfolks are going to nag their men no end. Even the most stubborn will get tired of hearing them jabber all day long, not counting at night, 'Water, water, water!' That'll start sounding like bells ringing and never stopping in their ears. 'Water, water, water!' until their own eyes begin to see visions of water running through the fields, of plants sprouting all by themselves. Then they'll say, 'All right, women, *oui*! It's all right, we agree!'

"As for me, I'll be responsible for the peasants on my side. I'll talk to them straight and they'll accept, I'm sure and certain. And I can see the day arrive when both sides will come face to face:

" 'Well, brothers,' " some will say, " 'are we brothers?' "

" 'Yes, we're brothers,' the others will reply. "

" 'Without a grudge?' "

" 'Without a grudge.' "

" 'Really?' "

" 'On with the *coumbite*?' "

" 'On with the *coumbite*!' "

"Ah!" she said, with an admiring smile. "How clever you are! I'm not intelligent, myself—but I'm crafty, too, *oui*. You'll see."

"You? You're smart as you can be, and I'll prove it. Answer this question—it's a riddle." With outstretched hand he pointed to the plain. "Do you see my hut? *Bueno.*

Now, follow me to the left, draw a straight line from the
mountain to that spot on the edge of the woods. *Bueno.*
That's a lovely location, isn't it? A man could build a hut
there with a railing, two doors, and maybe a small porch,
couldn't he? I can see the doors now, the windows, and the
railing all painted blue. Blue makes things look clean. In
front of the house, suppose a man planted bay trees. They're
not very useful, bay trees aren't. They give neither shade nor
fruit, but they'd just be there for decoration."

He put his arm around her shoulder and she trembled.
"Who'd be the mistress of that hut?"

"Let me alone," she said in a choked voice. "I'm warm."

"Who'd be the mistress of that garden?"

"Let me alone! Let me alone! I'm cold." She freed herself
of his embrace and stood up. She hung her head. She
wouldn't look at him. "It's time for me to go."

"You haven't answered my question, no."

She began to go down the slope, and he followed her.
She untied the horse's bridle.

"You haven't answered my question."

She turned toward Manuel, her face aglow. It wasn't a
ray of the setting sun, it was happiness. "Oh, Manuel!"

He held in his embrace the warm deep sweetness of her
body. "It's yes, Anna?"

"It's yes, darling. But let me go, please."

Touched by her plea, he let her slip from his arms.

"Well, goodbye, my master," she said, bowing.

"Goodbye, Anna."

With a graceful bound, she mounted her horse. One last
time she smiled at him. Then, spurring the animal with her
heel, she went down toward the ravine.

Chapter Seven

AS SHE APPROACHED Fonds Rouge, night began to envelop her, but the chestnut horse knew the road, having traversed it so often at this hour. Its regular pace lulled Annaise's thoughts. She was still upset by the languor that had gripped her, that astonishing surprise of the flesh, that sudden whirl of trees and sky before her frightened eyes, a dizzy spell that would have left her broken and confused in Manuel's arms, if her will power had not been snagged by a hidden panic.

She had lost her soul. Oh, God! Good Lord! What spell was this? Certain accursed people—I make the sign of the cross, protect me Gracious Virgin—know the evil charms that change a man into an animal, a plant into a rock in the twinkling of an eye, that's true, *oui*. I'm not the same any more. What's happened to me? It's a sweetness that almost hurts, a warmth that burns like ice. I'm giving in! I'm lost! Oh, Master of the Water, there's no bad magic in you, yet you know all the springs, even the one that lay dormant in the depths of my shame. You awakened it, and it's carrying me away. I can't resist, that's all. Here I am. You'll take my hand and I'll follow you. You'll take my body in your arms and I'll say, "Take me, I'll do your pleasure and your bidding." It's fate.

The horse reared all of a sudden. Someone or something had just leaped into the road.

"Who's there?" she cried, alarmed.

There was a rusty chuckle. "Good evening, cousin."

"Who's there? What's your name?"

"You don't recognize me?"

"How do you expect me to recognize you in this darkness?"

"It's me, Gervilen." He walked along beside her like a compact shadow, hardly different from the night, and she felt a vague threat in his presence. "So you were delayed in town?"

"Yes, the corn didn't sell well. And I don't know what's come over this horse to make him so mulish today. He's a nuisance, this horse!"

"Aren't you scared to go home after dark?"

"No, there aren't any criminals on this road."

"It's not highwaymen who are the most dangerous." And with the same sinister laugh, "There are, above all, evil spirits, demons, big devils, all kinds of Lucifers."

"God forgive me! St. James, St. Michael, help me!" she murmured, frightened.

"You're afraid?"

"My blood has turned to water."

Gervilen kept silent for a second, and during this silence Annaise suffered unbearable anxiety. "They say there's one around here."

"Where?"

"Do you want to know?"

"Oh, tell me quickly!"

He hissed, "On the mound where the macaw trees are!"

She understood immediately. Gervilen had spied on them, the evil-minded wretch, the Judas! With feigned indifference she said, "It might not be true."

"Anyhow, you didn't go that way, did you? That's not your road."

"No."

"You're lying!" He pulled so violently on the bridle that the chestnut horse reared and beat the air with its hoofs. He was yelling but his voice stuck deep in his throat, harsh and swollen with rage. She smelled his breath, poisoned by white rum. "You're lying, you shameless hussy! I saw you two with my own eyes."

"Let go of that bridle. You're drunk! I'm in a hurry to get home."

"Drunk? Are you going to claim that I didn't see him put his paws on you and you didn't do a thing to stop him?"

"And even if it is true, what right have you to meddle in my affairs? What authority have you got over me?"

"That's my business, damn it! We're from the same family. Isn't your mother, Rosanna, my dead mother's sister?"

"You smell like *tafia*," she said in disgust. "You make me sick at the stomach!"

"You're haughty all right, but you act like any prostitute. And with whom? With a good-for-nothing who has strayed off to foreign lands like a dog without a master—Bienaimé's son, Sauveur's nephew! I mean with our worst enemy of all!"

He spoke with bitter vehemence, but in a low voice, as if the night were listening. They were moving toward the flickering lights. Dogs began to bark. Back in the yards, silhouettes of peasants were stirring around reddish open-air kitchens.

"Annaise?"

She didn't answer.

"I'm talking to you, *oui*, Annaise."

"Haven't you finished cursing me?"

"That's because I was angry."

"So you are saying, excuse me?"

He muttered as though each word were being torn from him with pliers, "I say excuse me." He was still holding her horse by the bridle. "Annaise, have you thought about what I asked you the other day?"

"As far as that goes, *never*!"

"Is that your last word?"

"My very last."

"Then I don't need to send Dorismé, my uncle, to ask Rosanna for you?"

"No, it wouldn't be any use."

He spoke slowly, with a hoarse effort, as if he were strangling. "You'll be sorry, Annaise! And I swear, may the thunder turn me to ashes and the Virgin put out my eyes, if I don't get my revenge!"

In the darkness she imagined how twisted his face was. "You can't frighten me." But fear gripped her heart.

"I'm a man of my word. Mark well what I say—that Negro will regret ever having crossed the path of Gervilen Gervilis. Damn his soul!"

"What are you going to do?"

"Damn his soul, I say! Some day you'll understand these words, and you'll gnaw your fists to the bone!"

"Giddap!" he cried briskly to the horse, hitting its rump savagely with the flat of his hand.

The chestnut horse galloped off, and Annaise had trouble mastering it. When she got home, Rosanna was waiting for her. Rosanna was a huge Negro woman. She filled the entire doorway.

"Why are you so late getting back?"

Annaise dismounted, and Gille, her brother, advanced to unsaddle the horse.

"I'm talking to this girl! Can't she hear me?" demanded Rosanna angrily.

"Good evening, sister," Gille said. "She's asking you why you're so late getting home."

"Ah!" she groaned, at the end of her rope, "if you only knew how tired out I am!"

Chapter Eight

"YOU'RE WORRYING. You think I don't see it, but, *oui*, I do. I ask you why and you don't answer me. That's not right, son. No, that's not right. So you don't trust me? You've been like that ever since you were little—silent and shut up like a wall inside yourself whenever anybody tried to get near you. But there were times—Ah, Lord! one could say that it was only yesterday and yet so long a time has passed—there were times when you used to come close to me in the evening. 'Mama, tell me that story.' And I pretended to be busy and you'd say, 'Mama, please.' We'd be sitting in this very same place at nightfall, and I'd begin: 'Cric? Crac!' And finally you'd fall asleep with your head in my lap. That's how it was, son. It's your old mama who's telling you."

Délira put a piece of yam on Manuel's plate. That was all there was to eat today, with a bit of millet.

"You're talking drivel, wife," said Bienaimé.

"Perhaps, perhaps I am talking drivel. It's because there isn't much difference between then and now. Don't get mad, Manuel, if your old mama rambles a little.

"To me, you see, you're always just my little boy. And when you were lost in a foreign land, while I waited for you, I had a burden in my heart, just as if I were still carrying you in my stomach. It was the weight of pain. Ah, Manuel, what pain I suffered! And now you're back, but it's no better. No, and for several nights now I've had bad dreams."

Manuel ate in silence. His mother, seated on a stool at his feet, kept looking at him, her eyes drowned in sadness.

"Nothing's the matter with me, mama. I'm not sick, am I? Don't worry yourself."

"Of course you're not sick," Bienaimé interrupted. "Was there ever a bigger, stronger Negro? Délira, will you please leave him in peace, after all? Now, if I wanted to talk, too, I'd ask who taught him to handle a hoe and a pruning knife, to weed, to plant, and even to make traps to catch birds? I could run on like that forever." He lit his pipe with a firebrand.

"Have you finished eating?" Délira asked.

"Yes, I'm full up to here."

Bienaimé was lying. Hunger was gnawing his belly, but the old woman hadn't yet taken a mouthful, and there wasn't much left in the pot. As usual, he dragged his chair over to the calabash tree, and sat down facing the road. The sun crept about his feet, but his head was in the cool shade.

Délira humbly touched Manuel's arm. "Pardon, son, I say pardon for all these complaints. They're unfounded. But I've worried so much about you that my head keeps on turning around without anything in it. It turns and turns. It's really a mill of worries. When you go off to roam through those mountains, what you're seeking is a mystery. I watch you disappear behind the acacias, and suddenly my heart stops beating. Suppose he doesn't return? Suppose he goes away forever? I know that's impossible, but I pray to my angels and my saints as if there were some danger over your head. And at night I wake up and I open the door of your room, and I see you lying there. He's sleeping, he's breathing, he's there! Thanks, Virgin of the Miracles! It's because you're all I've got on this earth, son, and my old man—disagreeable as he is, poor old Bienaimé."

Manuel pressed her hand. He was deeply moved.

"Don't be upset about me, you hear, mama? And soon I'll tell you some great news, you hear, darling? I look worried because I expect it to happen every day and I'm impatient."

"What news, what event, what are you talking about, Manuel?"

"It's too soon to tell it. But it'll be something to be glad about, you'll see."

Délira looked at him, nonplussed. Then a tender smile erased whatever anxiety remained on her face. "You've chosen a girl? Ah, Manuel! It's time for you to settle down with a good hard-working *Négresse*, not one of those city hussies. How many times have I said to myself, 'I haven't long to live. Will I die without seeing my son's sons?' Tell me her name, because I've guessed right, haven't I? Wait: it's Marielle, no? Then, my old friend Clairemise's daughter, Célina. She's a nice girl, too."

"Neither of them, mama. And that's not the news, or rather—"

"Or rather?"

"That could be. In fact it's even certain. The two things are intertwined like the creepers and the branch. But don't ask me, mama. With all the respect that I owe you, it's still a secret because of the way things are."

"So you keep secrets from your own mother now." She was disappointed and somewhat embarrassed. "What's she like, that girl? Not one of those minxes, I hope."

"She's a *Négresse* who hasn't an equal in this whole country."

"What color is she? Is she black-black, or perhaps reddish?"

"Black-black. But you're going to ask me if she has large eyes or not, a nose like this or like that, or what size is she, whether she's fat or thin, whether she's a long-haired or a short-haired *Négresse*. Then you'd have her picture just as if she were standing right in front of you." He laughed. "Ah, mama, you're clever, *oui!*"

"All right, all right," said Délira, pretending to be provoked. "I'll shut my mouth. I don't want to know anything. I'm not meddling with anything. Get along, *m'sieur*, I've got these dishes to wash."

But you could see that the adventure intrigued and delighted her. Manuel put his arm around her neck and they both laughed. Délira's laugh was astonishingly young. That was because she hadn't had much chance to use it. Life isn't gay enough for that. No, she'd never had a chance to wear it out. She had kept it fresh like a bird's song in an old nest.

"Any one would think you two were lovers!" Bienaimé exclaimed. His uplifted arms called heaven to witness. "Just now she was groaning, and here she is laughing! What kind of comedy is this, *mes amis?* Women are as changeable as the weather. But that's *one* proverb that isn't true, for I'd certainly like a good rain to fall after all this dry spell." He drew on his pipe. "A cursed year like this I've never seen before."

The gray-tinted sky was a bare surface blurred by a hard sun-glare. Prostrate chickens looked for shade. The little dog was sleeping, his head between his paws. You could count his bones. If human beings had almost nothing to eat, just imagine the dogs!

Bienaimé closed his eyes. He was still holding his unlighted pipe, but his head dropped to one side. He was slipping off into that sleep which now overtook him at any hour in the day, and which often repeated the same dream: an enormous cornfield, leaves dripping with dew, ears of corn so swollen that they burst their husks with rows of kernels that seemed to be laughing.

As for Délira, she was washing the dishes, and she was singing. It was a song similar to life—it was sad. She knew no other. She wasn't singing aloud and it was a song without words, sung with closed lips. It stayed in her throat like a moan; yet her heart was eased since her chat with Manuel. Nevertheless, it knew no language other than this sorrowful plaint. She sang after the fashion of black women. Life has taught black women to sing as though they are choking back a sob, and it's a song that ends always with a beginning because it's in the image of misery. And does the circle of misery ever end?

If Manuel could read her thoughts, he'd object. He sees things in the light of joy, a glowing light. He says life is made so that men may have happiness and their contentment. Maybe he's right. Days come, days go, and some day that may be proven. But, meanwhile, life is hard.

For a long time, everything seemed to sleep. Only her song lulled the silence.

It was the Simidor's excited voice that awoke Bienaimé. "Bienaimé! Oh, Bienaimé I've got news," he said.

The old man yawned, rubbed his eyes, shook the ashes from his pipe. "More gossip that you're coming to tell me. If your legs moved as fast as your tongue, you'd make it from here to Port-au-Prince in the twinkling of an eye."

"No, what I'm telling you is the Lord's truth. Saint Julien's gone away. And brother Loctame, too."

"Well, they'll come back. A horse knows how long its rope is."

"But they've gone for good. Erzulie, Saint-Julien's wife, says they're going to cross the border over by Grand Bois and try to find work in the Dominican Republic. The poor woman's screaming and crying. Soon there won't be a single drop of water left in her body. Saint-Julien's left her with six young little Negroes. But what can you expect? This drought is discouraging. And some folks just can't resign themselves to dying. They prefer to leave the land of their ancestors, to try to make a living in a foreign country. And Charité, Sister Sylvina's daughter, has gone off, too."

"Is that so?"

"Yes, that's how it is, and others will surely follow after her. She's gone to the city. You know how she's going to end up? In sin and with the bad diseases. But it's better to be ugly than dead, the proverb says. And we're all going to die, if this keeps up. As far as I'm concerned, I ask nothing else. I'm old, I've lived my life. And what's the use of living anyhow if I can't sling my drum over my shoulder and lead a *coumbite* with my song, and drink my fill of *clairin* afterwards? I was born for that, with fingers like drumsticks and a flock of songbirds where my brain's supposed to be. So, I ask you, why am I still living? My role has ended."

The Simidor had been drinking a bit and, for once, liquor made him bitter.

"Jesus-Virgin!" Délira sighed. "If the young folks leave, who then will bury our old bones so that on Judgment Day, between Satan and the Eternal Father, they can be put together?"

"You get on my nerves, Délira," Bienaimé growled. "And the Good Lord's going to get tired of hearing you call his name every time you say *yes* or *no*." He turned to Antoine. "You've got to keep them from leaving. This soil has fed us for generations. It's still good. All it wants is a little water. Tell them the rain will come, to have patience. No, I'll go and tell them myself."

But would the peasants listen to Bienaimé? They were fed up with poverty. They were worn out. The most reasonable among them were losing their senses. The strongest were wavering. As for the weak, they had given up. "What's the use?" they said. One could see them stretched out, sad and silent, on pallets before their huts, thinking about their hard luck, stripped of all their will power. Others were spending their last pennies on *clairin* at Florentine's, the wife of the rural policeman, or else they were buying it on credit, which would sooner or later catch up with them. Alcohol gave them a semblance of vigor, a brief illusion of hope, a momentary forgetfulness. But they would wake up stormy-headed and dry-mouthed. Life would take on the taste of vomit then, and they wouldn't even have a piece of salt meat to settle the stomach.

Fonds Rouge was falling away into debris, and the debris consisted of these good peasants, these earnest hardworking Negroes of the land. Wasn't it a pity, after all?

"Manuel! Where is that Manuel?" Bienaimé cried.

"He's gone out," Délira replied.

"Always gone, always out! Always gadding about in the mountains. Wild roving Negro, that son of yours, Délira."

"He's your son, too, Bienaimé."

"Don't cross me! He must've got that from you."

"Yes, because you're beyond reproach, you are!"

"I'm not saying that. It would be boasting."

"There are some," the Simidor remarked, "whose backsides are light as kites—they just can't keep still. It's not their fault."

But Délira was angry. When that happened—and it was rare—she would draw up her fleshless body and seem very tall. Her voice didn't rise. It remained calm and deliberate, but the words cut like knives.

"That's right. I've been a gadabout. I haven't worked for you all the days of my life, from sunup to dark of night. I've done nothing but laugh and dance. Poverty hasn't scratched my face—look at these wrinkles! Poverty hasn't burned me—look at my hands! Poverty hasn't bled me dry—if only you could see inside my heart! As for you, you're a Negro without a fault, a Negro without equal, a Negro beyond compare! Thank you, Lord, that a person of so little merit should be the wife of a man like him!"

"All right! Enough, I say! Enough, woman! Enough for my ears! Brother Antoine, let's go out and see what's going on."

Watching them move off, Délira shook her head and smiled. Her anger had vanished. "Ah! Bienaimé! Ah! my poor dear!" she whispered.

Her thoughts returned at once to Manuel. What can he be seeking in those mountains? Maybe a treasure? The idea struck her suddenly. White Frenchmen had lived in these parts. Here and there one could still see traces of their indigo factories. And didn't folks say that a peasant from Boucan Corail had found by chance, while digging in his fields, a jar filled with pieces of silver money? What was that peasant's name? Oh, pshaw! I've forgotten, but that doesn't matter. The story was true. Bienaimé had seen one of the coins. It was as big as that and heavy! An Italian in the city had paid a good price for it, and the peasant—what was his name? Ciriaque, that was it! Ciriaque had bought some ground over by Mirebalais and had become a big landowner.

"But they say that to find a treasure you have to make a bargain with the devil. Manuel couldn't do that. I'm sure not!"

That Chambrun plateau, where Manuel was then, arose in the midst of a small plain, isolated, like an island from the waves of the surrounding hills. From there the eye could survey the entire countryside. On the east, the promontory whence rose the smoke was Bellevue. Those huts down there, Boucan Corail. And farther, in the distant blue, like shelves on a gentle slope, Mahotière and its lovely truck gardens in the shade of mango and avocado trees. Its peasants were even lucky enough to have a spring of good drinking water, which also sufficed for washing clothes. It spurted in a gorge where carib cabbage grew, and watercress, and even mint. That was where the Fonds Rouge folks got their water now—but it was far, and the filled calabashes were heavy on the way back.

Above Mahotière, after about a day's ride, one reached Morne Villefranche where the pine forests began on its hillsides, with long veils of fog, humid rags worse than rain, penetrating to the marrow of your bones. It was a high mountain, torn by bottomless chasms, crowned by peaks that were lost in the unsettled sky. The trees there were black and solemn and the wind wailed night and day through their branches, for pines are sensitive and musical.

Before Manuel's gaze the crest of the mountains ran to the west in a single pale blue wave soothing to the eye. If sometimes the hollow of a valley like Chambrun plateau broke it, it soon swept up again with a new surge of more red gum trees, more oaks, and the same tangled brush through which the macaw trees shot.

The stirring of a quick silky breeze made him look up toward a flock of passing wood pigeons. "They're the large gray variety." He followed their ashen path until they swooped down one by one on a nearby hill.

Suddenly an idea struck him that jerked him bolt upright Wood pigeons preferred cool places. ¡*Caramba*! Suppose this were a sign from heaven?

He went back down the hill almost at a run. His heart was beating furiously. "What's happening to you, Manuel?" he asked himself. "One would think that you were going to your first rendezvous with a girl. Your blood's on fire!"

A strange uneasiness knotted his throat. "I'm afraid it'll be like the other times, a delusion, a deception, and I feel that if I don't find it this time I'll be discouraged. Maybe I'll even say, 'Well, all right, I give up.' No, it isn't possible! Can a man desert the soil? Can he turn his back on it? Can he divorce it without losing the very reason for his existence, the use of his hands, the taste for life?"

Yes, he'd begin his search again, he was sure of that. It was his mission and his duty. Those Fonds Rouge peasants, those hardheaded, rock-headed peasants needed that water to bring about friendship between brothers again and to make life over as it ought to be—an act of good will between men, by want and fate made equals.

He crossed the drain of the plain. He walked rapidly. He was in a hurry, impatient, for it seemed to him that his blood had congealed in his throat and was doing its best to escape through a dull deep thumping in his heart.

"That's where the wood pigeons have roosted—in that thick-wooded mountain. There are even mahogany trees there. And that grayish foliage that looks silver in the sun— if I'm not mistaken those are trumpet trees. And naturally there are plenty of gum trees. But which side should I take to get there?"

His ear guided him, more so than his eye. With each step that he took with the aid of his machete through the maze of plants and vines, he expected to hear the frightened pigeons fly away. He cut through the forest obliquely, toward the thickest part of the mountain. He had already noted this retreat, this darkened wood where the trees were clustered in a turbid light. A steep gully opened before him. He descended, holding on to the bushes. The stones which rolled under him, immediately aroused an intense flapping of wings. The wood pigeons broke loose from the branches and, through the opening in the foliage, he saw them disperse in all directions.

"They were higher. Some were on that giant fig tree over there."

Manuel was at the bottom of a kind of narrow gully encumbered by creeping vines which fell weeping from the trees. A cool breeze blew and that may have been why the twining unruly plants grew so tough and so close together. He went up toward the giant fig tree. He felt the blessed breeze dry his sweat. He was walking through a great silence.

Then, he entered a deep green shade, and his last machete stroke revealed the mountain circling a wide level space where the giant fig tree proudly lifted its powerful trunk. Its branches, laden with floating moss, covered the spot with venerable shade, and its monstrous roots extended an authoritative hand over the ownership and secret of this corner of the earth.

Manuel stopped. He scarcely believed his eyes. A sort of weakness struck his knees. It was because he saw *malangas*. He even touched one of their broad, smooth, icy leaves. And *malangas* are plants that always accompany water!

His machete plunged into the earth. He dug furiously, and the hole was not yet deep or large before water began to creep up through the chalk-white soil. He began again farther on, attacked the *malangas* in a frenzy, pulling out whole armfuls, tearing them out by the fistful. Each time there was a bubbling which turned into a small puddle that looked like a bright eye as soon as it had settled.

Manuel lay down on the ground. With his whole body he embraced the earth.

"There she is! The good, sweet, flowing, singing, cooling, blessed life!"

He kissed the earth with his lips and laughed.

Chapter Nine

"HAVE YOU NOTICED our Manuel? For two days he's been acting as if he had fallen into a nest of ants. He's here, he's there, but never in the same place. He goes out to the road, sits down on the porch, and then gets up again. You call him, he doesn't hear. You call him again, and he seems to come out of a dream. 'Eh, yes?' he says, but you can see that he's not listening to you. At night I hear him twisting and turning on his mattress, turning and tossing. He's looking for sleep and can't find it. Early this morning, I heard him laughing all by himself while he was bathing behind the house. Could he be losing his mind, our boy? Bienaimé, my man, answer me, Bienaimé."

"How do you expect me to answer you?" the old man replied ill-humoredly. "I'm not in his skin. I'm not in his head. He's an active fellow, that Manuel, a restless Negro, that's all. Some folks are slow by nature, and others are quick as lightning. What do you find so strange and upsetting about that? You'd like to have him always in the folds of your dress like a little boy, and you'd like him to say, 'Mama, this hurts! Mama, that hurts!' as if he hadn't grown up, as if he weren't a big strong man, with all his senses and his own mind. So let him have his freedom. Young colts are made to gallop across the savanna. Give me a piece of charcoal to light my pipe."

"Weren't you complaining the other day about his always running around?"

"*Me*? When was that?" The old man feigned astonishment. "Are you trying to pick a fuss with me, Délira?"

"And what about that shovel he bought in town yesterday? Can you tell me why he needs it? And why he took it with him this morning to the mountains? And why, on his return, it was all covered with some kind of white soil, the like of which isn't around here?"

"How do you expect me to answer all those whys? Ask me once and for all the reason the moon sometimes resembles a slice of Spanish melon, when at other times it's as round as a dish. The fact is, you're aggravating, *oui*, Délira. Why are you pinching my sides with your questions the whole day? When you were a young girl, you were on the untalkative side—it was hard to get a word out of you. To tell you the truth, I regret the past."

He buried himself in his chair, grumbling and vexed, his lips squeezing his pipestem. His troubles were increasing. When a man begins to have bad luck, they say, even a curd of clabber can break his head. The spotted heifer had gotten entangled in her rope and had sprained a leg. Dorméus had charged three *gourdes* to treat her, the scoundrel! But she was slow in mending and Bienaimé would have to wait still longer now before selling her. Lhérisson had gone away to work at Croix des Bouquets with a gang from the Department of Public Works. Others were thinking of following his example, and even of leaving Fonds Rouge for good. And now, Manuel was acting like he was about to take down with epilepsy! When, by the beard of the Holy Ghost!—pardon, Lord, I've blasphemed, I won't do it any more, *mea culpa*—when will all these goddamn troubles end?

But here comes Sister Destine. How does she manage to keep so fat? Bienaimé wondered. Her big black face was shining like waxed leather.

"Just stopping to bid you good day, Sister Délira. Brother Bienaimé, good day, *oui*."

"Good day, honey!" the old man replied. Then he pretended to be asleep. He was not anxious to talk. Délira, still standing, had pushed up a stool for Destine. Destine sprawled all over it, jutting out on all sides.

"How's life?" she asked.

"Our penance continues," Délira sighed. With a nod of her head, she pointed toward the fields, then she raised her eyes to the implacable sky. It was the hottest moment of the day, yet it wasn't noon, but rather about two o'clock. The earth had begun to exude a vapor that danced and made the eyes squint, it was so blinding.

In the acacia trees, a melancholy dove cooed. The male answered her with a harsh call. But their dialogue did not break the silence. It accompanied it and made it more oppressive and immediate.

"I'm going away, too," Destine declared.

"Don't say that!" Délira exclaimed, alarmed.

"Yes, dear, that's how it is. We're going to leave the land of our ancestors, my man Joachim and I. We've got relatives at Boucan Corail, distant relatives, but maybe they'll be charitable and give us a small piece of land—enough to build a hut on and plant a little garden. It's God's will, Délira, but how bad I feel!"

She was weeping. The tears traced soiled lines down her cheeks.

Life had dried up at Fonds Rouge. One had only to listen to this silence to hear death. One yielded to this torpor and felt himself already buried. The regular and repeated blows of the mallets in the mortars had become stilled since there wasn't a grain of millet to husk. How far things were from the good old days of the *coumbite*, from the virile joyous chant of the menfolk, from the sparkling, swinging hoes in the sun, from those happy years when we used to dance the minuet under the arbors with the carefree voices of dark young girls bursting forth like a fountain in the night!

Adieu, I say, *adieu* to the days of pardon and mercy! *Adieu, adieu*, we're leaving, it's ended. Oh, *loas*, my *loas* of Guinea, you don't weigh the work of our hands according to our share of misery. Your scales are false. That's why we're dying with no help and with no hope. Is it fair? Answer me!

No, truly it's not fair!

Délira said in a tranquil voice, "On All Saints' Day, I cleaned up the graves of my dead relatives. They're all buried here, they're waiting for me. My day is beginning to end, my night is approaching. I can't go away."

Destine was still weeping. "I've got two sons in the cemetery."

Délira touched her on the shoulder. "Take heart, Destine. You'll come back, cousin. You'll come back with the rain and the good season."

Destine wiped her eyes with the back of her soft, fat, seemingly boneless hand. "This morning there was a snake curled around the beam of our hut. Joachim got up on the table and chopped its head off with his pruning knife. 'Joachim,' I said, 'I only hope that doesn't bring us bad luck, do you hear me, Joachim?' But he shrugged his shoulders without a word.

"This situation is eating Joachim, eating him on the inside like a disease so that now he scarcely ever opens his mouth. And Florentine keeps demanding what's due her for *clairin*, with all kinds of threats and vile words that can't be repeated—that slut, that policeman's hussy!"

She got up. "We'll see each other again, Délira, sweet. I'm not leaving before the end of the week. I met Manuel on the road. My! but he's a fine boy! You're lucky, cousin. My two boys are in the cemetery. But that's life. You can't do much about bad luck. You just have to bear it."

After she had left, Bienaimé opened his eyes. He see-sawed his chair forward, and stamped angrily.

"Ah! You ungrateful Negroes!" he cried. "This soil has fed you day after day for years. Now you leave it with a few laments for the sake of appearances, and a little water in your eyes as if to wash off your guilty conscience and remorse. Band of hypocrites! As for us, we're staying! Aren't we, Délira? Aren't we, old woman?"

"Where on earth could we go?" Délira answered.

Finally, after two impatient days, Manuel had succeeded in finding her. She was walking along the road in plain view of the huts. But he had whispered to her as he passed, whispered between his teeth, "Wait for me under the tamarind tree down by Brother Lauriston's fence."

Now he was leading her toward the spring. She had difficulty in following him, so fast did he travel. She was afraid, too, that someone would see her. But Manuel reassured her that this place had been abandoned for a long time. It was an old cotton field alongside the thorn acacias.

"Look! It's full of weeds and prickles now."

They entered the woods. The sun shimmered through the mesh of the trees and rippled along the path with the movement of the wind in the tall branches.

"Do you believe there's enough water?" Annaise asked.

"I dug *that* deep." With his hand he pointed to his waist. "And not just one hole, either. Several. All along the plateau. It's full, a great basin, I tell you." He was out of breath, less on account of their rapid pace than because of his memory. "If I hadn't stopped up the holes again, I think they would have overflowed, there's so much of it."

"You're smart, *oui*, Manuel"

"No, it's just that I have faith."

"Faith in what?"

"Faith in life, Anna. Faith that men can't die."

She reflected a second. "What do you mean? They're just like that water—your words. I have to dig down deep to find their meaning."

"Naturally the day comes when each man must enter the earth. But life itself is a thread that doesn't break, that can't be lost. Do you know why? Because every man ties a knot in it during his lifetime with the work that he does—that's what keeps life going through the centuries—man's work on this earth."

She looked at him fervently. "Jesus-Mary-Virgin! How wise you are! And all those ideas, do they come out of your own head?" She began to laugh. "Don't you get a headache sometimes?"

"So you're trying to make fun of me, huh?" He took her by the arms and immediately Anna's expression changed. The light wavered in her eyes and she said in a choked voice, because her heart was beating in her throat, "Lead me to the spring."

The thicket grew clearer. The trees were now farther apart. At the end of the path, the open spaces of the plain appeared.

"You see that mountain?" Manuel asked. "No, not that one, the other—the wooded, dark blue one just under that cloud? That's where it is. Wait, I'm going to see if anyone's coming."

He went out of the woods, glanced around, then signaled to her and she joined him.

"Let's go quickly, Manuel. I'm afraid somebody'll see us."

She didn't tell him that since their meeting on the macaw mound, Gervilen had been spying on her. At the bend of a road, he would suddenly appear. He wouldn't say anything, but his bloodshot eyes would have a sinister gleam. Today he had gone to town. That she knew because her brother, Gille, was to accompany him there as a witness before the justice of the peace. It had something to do with a mule stolen or strayed—she no longer remembered which.

Gille had asked her, "Have you had an argument with Cousin Gervilen? Night before last when he came to see me, he looked at you mighty funny." She hadn't answered.

"You seem to be in a dream," Manuel said. "You're not saying anything, sweetheart."

"I wish we were there. We've been a long time getting across the plain. I feel eyes on my back. It's just like the prick of a knife."

Manuel looked in all directions. "Don't be scary! There's nobody around. Soon we won't have to hide. Everybody will know for whom I'm going to build a hut. Three rooms it will have, three. I've already figured it out. The furniture I'm going to make myself. There's some nice mahogany around these parts, and I'm something of a carpenter. And there'll be an arbor, too, with a climbing vine for shade. We might try grapes, what do you think? With a lot of coffee grounds about the roots, they'll grow, don't you think so?"

"That will be as you wish," she whispered.

Yes, I'll be the mistress of your hut, I'll sow your fields, and I'll help you bring in the harvest. I'll go out in the dew at sunrise to gather the fruits of our soil. In the evening afterglow, I'll go and see if the chickens are resting on the tree branches, if the wild and savage beasts haven't carried them off. I'll take our corn and provisions to market. You'll await my return on the doorstep. The lamplight will be behind you on the table, but I'll hear your voice, "Did you have a good sale, wife?" And I'll answer according to the good way or bad way things went that day. I'll serve your meals and remain standing while you eat. And you'll say, "Thanks, sweetheart." And I'll reply, "At your service, my master," for I'll be the servant of your household. At night I'll lie at your side. You'll say nothing, but I'll respond to your silences, to the pressure of your hand, "*Oui*, my man," for I'll be the servant of your desire. There'll be a stream of water in our garden with reeds and laurels on its banks. You've promised me that. And there'll be children that I'll give you. That I promise in the name of the saints who are on earth, in the name of the saints who are in the stars!

Her face reflected the gravity of her soul.

"Your brows are knitted," Manuel exclaimed. "Your eyes are peering off into the distance. Tell me what's wrong, sweetheart."

She smiled at him but her mouth was trembling. "Where's the spring, Manuel?"

"We're there now. Give me your hand. There's a climb that isn't easy."

They followed the road hacked out by Manuel's machete through the stifling plants. Manuel went down first into the gully. She hesitated, slipped a bit, and he caught her in his arms. Against his body he felt the weight and warmth of hers. But she freed herself.

"It smells cool," she said. "It smells like wind and water."

The wood pigeons took to the wing, opening a passage through the leaves toward the sky. She lifted her eyes toward the branches which closed again on the silence.

"It's dark! How dark it is! You wouldn't think there was a great sun outside. Here it filters down drop by drop. I listen, I hear no sound. It's just like we were on a little island. We're far away, Manuel, we're at the very end of the world."

"At the beginning of the world, you mean. Because at the beginning of beginnings, there were a woman and a man like you and me. The first spring flowed at their feet, and the woman and the man entered the spring and bathed in life." He took her hand. "Come!" He pushed the vines aside. She walked in the mysterious shade of the giant fig tree.

"That's the keeper of the water," she whispered in a sort of sacred terror. "He's the keeper of the water." She looked at the branches laden with silvery, floating moss. "He's terribly old."

"He's terribly old."

"You can't see his head."

"His head's in the sky."

"His roots are like feet."

"They hold the water."

"Show me the water, Manuel."

He dug in the soil. "Look!"

She knelt down, wet a finger in the pool and made the sign of the cross.

"I greet you, holy water!" she said.

"And there, look again! It's everywhere!"

"I see it," she said. She put her ear to the ground. "I hear it."

She listened, with her quiet face lighted by an infinite joy. He was beside her.

"Anna!"

Their lips touched.

"My sweet," she sighed.

She closed her eyes and he laid her down. She was stretched out on the ground and the low rumble of the water echoed within her in a sound that was the tumult of her own blood. She didn't defend herself. His hand, so heavy, transmitted an intolerable sweetness.

"I'm going to die!"

Beneath his touch, her body burned. He unlocked her knees, and she opened herself to him. He entered, a lacerating presence, and she gave an injured groan.

"No! Don't leave me—or I'll die!"

Her body went to meet his in a feverish surge. In her an unspeakable anguish was born, a terrible delight which absorbed the movements of her body. A panting wail rose to her lips.

Then she felt herself melt in the deliverance of that long sob that left her prostrate in man's embrace.

Chapter Ten

"THE SUN'S RISING," Délira said.

"It's hit the mountain," Bienaimé observed.

The chickens were cackling uneasily. They were waiting for someone to toss them some corn, but the peasants had nothing left to eat themselves, or almost nothing. They held on to the last grains, crushed them under the mallet and made a thick, heavy soup, but it was filling. It gave body to one's stomach. The cocks confronted each other, a ruff of feathers bristling about their necks. They exchanged a few pecks, a few blows of their spurs.

"Shhhh!" When Bienaimé clapped his hands together, they separated to make a stand farther on, and to crow their full-throated defiance.

It's like that in every yard. Thus day begins, with a light that can't make up its own mind, drowsy trees, and smoke rising behind the huts—for it's coffee time. And it isn't a bad idea to dip a piece of cracker in it if the coffee is well sweetened—with cane syrup, of course, because sugar, even brown sugar, the cheap kind, simply can't be had these days.

"Manuel said he was going to look for Laurélien."

"That's what he *said*."

"But what's going on, Bienaimé?"

"Ask me all you like, I'll not answer."

"It's been a long time since I heard an agreeable word out of your mouth."

Bienaimé gulped a swallow of coffee. He felt ashamed. "That's because my rheumatism's starting up again," he said to excuse himself. "Suppose you rub me with a little oil? It's got me in the joints."

"I'll heat the oil with some salt. That'll penetrate the pain better."

The old man lighted his pipe. He caressed his white beard. "Délira, ho!"

"Yes, Bienaimé?"

"I want to tell you something."

"I'm listening, *oui*, Bienaimé."

"You're a good wife, Délira." He turned his head and cleared his throat. "And I'm going to tell you something else."

"Yes, dear?"

"I'm a disagreeable Negro."

"No, Bienaimé, no, my man! You just have your bad days. It's the fault of all this misery. But since we've been walking together through life—and it's been a long road, God knows! with so many rough places and plenty of tribulations—you've always protected me, you've supported me, you've helped me. I've leaned on you, and I've been sheltered."

But the old man insisted, "I tell you I'm a disagreeable Negro!"

"I know you inside and out. There isn't a better man anywhere."

"You're contrary, *oui*, Délira! I swear I've never seen a more stubborn woman than you are."

"Good, Bienaimé, that's right."

"What's right, what?"

"You *are* a disagreeable Negro."

"*Me?*" said Bienaimé, disconcerted and furious.

Délira gave her clear little laugh. "You're the one that says so."

"But you don't need to repeat it. The entire neighborhood will hear it. 'Bienaimé's a disagreeable Negro, Bienaimé's a . . .' Well, *oui*, and so what?" Anger was the only sap that remained in his veins. He made full use of it.

Manuel and Laurélien approached with long strides. They were coming out of the woods. They were laughing, and Laurélien, usually so calm, was pounding Manuel's shoulder with blows heavy enough to cripple an ox.

"He's found it!" he shouted from afar. "He's found it!"

"What's that Laurélien yelling about? He's gone crazy, no?" Bienaimé grumbled. "Here he comes prancing as though he were walking on prickles! Has he been drinking so early this morning?"

Délira went to get some chairs.

"At your service!" said Laurélien touching his forehead.

"Hello, son," the old man replied. He looked at him suspiciously. "Absinthe," he said, "shouldn't be abused. One glassful to wake up your stomach I don't mind, but no more."

"I'm drunk, that's the truth," Laurélien laughed. He was twisting his huge hands and chuckling. "Yet I haven't had a drop, not even *that* much! Délira, how's life? Ah, my good sister, life's going to change from today on! It's going to change." He turned toward Manuel. His face grew serious. "Speak, Chief. Tell them about it!"

"It's about water," Manuel began. He was breathing hard. Each word was charged with emotion. "Since I returned to Fonds Rouge, I've been searching for it." He opened his arms, his face was full of sunlight. He almost shouted, "I've found it! A big spring, a basin full to overflowing, able to irrigate the whole plain. Everybody'll have all he needs and plenty left over."

Bienaimé leaped to his feet. His trembling hand clutched Manuel's shirt.

"You did that? You found water? Is it true?" He was laughing with a peculiar expression on his face. His voice broke and tears were flowing into his white beard. "Respect, my son! Your papa's telling you 'respect,' because you're a great Negro. Yes, hats off to you, Manuel Jean-Joseph! Délira, do you hear? My boy's found water! By himself, with his own hands. I recognize my blood. I recognize my race. That's the way we are in this family—enterprising Negroes—and we don't lack intelligence either!" He wouldn't release Manuel. He stammered, his eyes clouded, "Ah, son, son!"

Délira pressed her hands against her heart. She was staring at Manuel, but saying nothing. She felt as weak as she had on the day that he came into the world. She had been weeding the fields when the pains struck. She had dragged herself to her hut, bitten her cries in the flesh of her forearm, and he was born from an immense laceration of her being. She herself had cut the cord, washed and laid the infant down in clean cloths before sinking into black unconsciousness, until Bienaimé's voice and the womenfolk's chatter had aroused her. Today, he was here before her, this man so tall, so strong, with that light on his forehead, this man who knew the mystery of water sleeping in the veins of the mountains!

He was beside her. His arms were fondling her shoulders. He was asking, "Are you happy, mama?"

She heard a voice answer, far, far away, yet it was her own, "I'm happy for us, I'm happy for the soil, I'm happy for the growing things." The world went reeling around her, the hut, the trees, the sky. She had to sit down.

Bienaimé plied Manuel with questions. "Tell me about it, son. Where is this water? What's it like?" And, with a sudden worry, "It isn't just a little bit of water, is it? A trickle next to nothing, only good enough to drink?"

"No," Manuel replied. "It's a lot of water! You should see the place—a big shelf of earth white as chalk. That kind of soil drinks up water easily, but down deeper, the water must have found something harder, more resistant, so it collected there. I'll bet in a few years it would have overflowed. Now, what we've got to do first is plant a row of poles close together to hold the soil, because if we begin by digging in the basin, it will be just like cracking a pitcher—the water will flood in all directions. Afterward, we'll dig the main canal down through the plain past the acacias, and in every little field each one of us will have his own ditch for his own irrigation. When the main canal and the others are ready, we'll open up the basin. It would be a good idea to appoint a trustee, too, somebody that all the peasants believe in, to distribute the water according to what each peasant needs. You see, it's a big job."

"The trustee will be you, Chief," Laurélien said. "It's already voted."

"Do you hear him, Délira?" Bienaimé exclaimed with great pride. "He's already figured it all out in his head. What he says is reason itself." But a thought seemed to disturb his joy all of a sudden. "You said, 'All the peasants.' You don't include . . . those *others*?"

Manuel was expecting that question. "Can I speak frankly and truthfully?" he asked. "And are you listening to me? Mama? Brother Laurélien?"

"We're listening, *oui*, Manuel."

"Good! How many able-bodied men do we have on our side? Wait!" He counted on his fingers. "Fourteen. And the others, the heirs and partisans of the dead Dorisca, are probably about the same number. Papa, mama, just think! Brother Laurélien, figure that out. Alone, we'd never get all that work done—poles to be cut, carried, planted. A long canal across the plain, and the forest to clear so that it can pass. And besides, water isn't something that can be divided up into acres. It can't be marked out on a notary's paper—it's everybody's, the blessing of the earth! What right would we have . . . ?"

Bienaimé didn't let him finish. "The right that *you* found it!" he cried. "The right that our enemies haven't got any rights!" He made an effort to control himself. "But tell me straight out what you mean to do."

"To go and find the others. 'Brothers,' I'll tell them, 'it's true what they're saying, *oui*, brothers. I've found a spring that can water all the fields of the plain. But to bring it here, we need everyone's help—a general *coumbite*, that's what it'll take. What one hand can't do, two can. Let's lend each other a hand. I come to propose peace and reconciliation. What do any of us gain in being enemies? If you want an answer, look at your children! Look at your growing things—death is on them. Misery and desolation ravage Fonds Rouge. So let your better judgment have a voice. Yes, blood has been shed, I know, but water will wash the blood away. The new crop will grow out of the past and ripen in forgetfulness. There's only one way to save ourselves—only *one*, not two. It's for us to make again one good family of peasants, to call together again in the name of brother to brother our union of tillers of the soil, to share our pain and our labor between comrades and comrades . . .' "

"Shut your big trap, speechifier!" Bienaimé roared. "I'm not going to listen any more. Keep on, and I'll tan your hide all up and down your back with a club."

He broke his pipe, throwing it violently on the ground. Across the fields he went to give air and space to his rage.

Bienaimé's fury surprised the others like a sudden downpour. They kept silent. Délira sighed. Laurélien lifted his heavy hands and scanned them as though they were strange tools. Manuel had that stubborn pucker at the corner of his mouth.

"Mama," he said finally, "what do you think about all that?"

"Ah, son! you're asking me to choose between you and Bienaimé."

"No, just between right and wrong—it's a matter of life or death."

Délira struggled with herself, that could be seen from her indecisive look. The words stopped at her lips. Her fingers tormented the cord of her scapulary. But there was nothing she could do but answer, "Dorisca and Sauveur are already ashes and dust. For years they've been resting in peace. Time passes, life goes on. I wore heavy mourning for Sauveur. He was my brother-in-law, and a good man. But there never has been a place for hatred in the heart of Délira Délivrance, may the Good Lord hear me!"

"And you, Laurélien?"

"I'm with you, Chief. The only way out of this situation is to make up. And the others will agree, too, if you talk to them the right way. I've never seen a man cleverer with his tongue than you are. That's right, *oui*!"

Bienaimé was leaning against the gate. He turned his back to them, indicating his refusal.

Manuel said, "For a long time Fonds Rouge has had a rotten smell. Hate poisons a person's breath. It's like a stagnant pool of green mud, of cooked bile, of spoiled, rancid, mortifying souls. But now that water's going to irrigate the plain, that it's going to flow in the fields, he who was an enemy will become a friend. He who was apart will unite, and peasants will no longer act like mad dogs to other peasants. Each man will recognize his equal, his likeness, and his neighbor. And here's the strength of my arm if you need it to work your fields and if you knock at my door saying, 'Honor,' I'll answer, 'Respect, brother! Come in and have a seat. My food is ready. Eat, you're more than welcome!' "

"That's the living truth," Laurélien approved.

"I know my folks," Manuel continued. "Their heads are harder and more stubborn than millet under the mallet. But if a man won't think with his head, he'll think with his belly—especially if it's empty. That's how I'll get to them, in their most sensitive spot. I'm going to see them and talk to them one after the other. You can't swallow a bunch of grapes all at once, no. But grape by grape it's easy."

"But, there're still those others," said Délira uneasily.

"The dead Dorisca's folks?"

"Yes, son."

Manuel smiled. "You say 'those others' as if they were a bunch of devils. Well, mama, I tell you, just between us, the day isn't far off when there'll be neither 'those others' nor 'ourselves,' but just good peasants gathered together for the great *coumbite* of the water."

"I don't know how you're going to do it—but be careful, *oui*. Night before last, I heard a noise out in the yard. I got up and opened the door ajar. There was a full moon. The man must have heard the key turn in the lock, because he started leaving. I only saw his back, but from his size and his walk it was surely Gervilen. I'd swear it—if that wasn't a sin."

Manuel shrugged his shoulders indifferently. "Probably drunk. He'd lost his way, that's all."

He had spoken to Gervilen only once, in the thorny acacia woods the day following his return to Fonds Rouge. Since then, Manuel had no trouble with him, except recently at a cockfight when he had stared at him peculiarly with eyes like red coals. But he was obviously as full of white rum as a demijohn, the poor fool!

"Manuel's right," said Laurélien. "That Gervilen's a drunken Negro. *Tafia* must have gone to his head and he got lost in your yard like a chicken thief."

But Délira didn't seem too convinced. The man she had seen wasn't staggering. He was walking straight and quickly toward the gate.

Laurélien shook Manuel's hand. "I'm going to spread the news, but as far as this matter of making up is concerned, that's for you to talk to them about."

"*Bueno,*" said Manuel. "I'll see them later."

"At your service, Délira," said Laurélien politely.

"*Adieu,* Laurélien," the old woman answered. She made an effort to get up. "What's come over me? I feel like I've been run through the mill. I haven't got any more strength."

Manuel restrained her. "Wait a little while."

"What is it, son?"

"The other day you wanted to know that girl's name, didn't you? Well, I'm going to tell you. It's Annaise."

"Rosanna's daughter?" Délira cried.

"Herself. But you look like you're bowled over."

"That's because it can't be, Manuel. Just think, we're enemies."

"In a few days there won't be any more enemies in Fonds Rouge."

"And do you think Bienaimé will agree?"

"Of course. Naturally, he'll get mad first. But he'll be the one who'll take the proposal letter to Rosanna. Tomorrow I'm going to buy it in town as well as the green silk handkerchief to wrap it in, since that's the way proper folks do things. I've still got to find somebody to write it for me, though. I'm no good at that. Do you have any suggestions?"

"At the left of the church in town, on the market place, there's a two-story house with a tin roof. Ask for *M'sieur* Paulma and say Sister Délira sent you. He's a fat mulatto who keeps a hardware store. You'll find him behind the counter. He knows writings."

She smiled almost dreamily. "Ah, Manuel! You've chosen a pretty girl, and she's serious and hard-working, so I've heard. I've seen her grow up. And before all that Dorisca-Sauveur fuss, she used to help me carry my calabashes when I came back from the spring. 'Aunty,' she used to call me, that's what she used to call me. She was a very respectful young girl, that Annaise. I'll get down on my knees, if I have to, before my old Bienaimé to beg him not to be contrary, and I'll pray to the Virgin of the Miracles. I'll say, 'Give your aid to my children. Put your hand on their heads and protect them from misfortune, and guide their steps in life, for life is hard and misery is great for us poor peasant folks.' "

"Thanks, mama, dear mama!" said Manuel. He dropped his head to hide his feelings.

"When you've finished plotting with him, Délira, you can go and buy me another pipe at Florentine's." It was Bienaimé returning. He didn't seem any too agreeable, Bienaimé didn't. That was apparent from the way he bit off his words.

"Yes, Bienaimé," Délira hastened to say, "*oui*, papa, I'm going right away."

Before noon, the rumor that Manuel had discovered a spring had spread throughout the village. We have a word for that, we Negroes of Haiti, "the tell-a-mouth" we call it. That's all it takes for a report, good or bad, true or false, agreeable or disagreeable, to circulate from mouth to mouth, from door to door, and soon it's gone all over the country. You'd be astonished at how fast it works.

And since Fonds Rouge wasn't very large, it had spread as quickly as a fire in dry grass. By the time the sun reached its zenith over the plain, the peasants were talking only about this event, some guaranteeing that it was true, others that it was not. Some went so far as to affirm that Manuel had brought back a magic wand from Cuba that could discover streams—and even hidden treasures. In short, each one added a bit of salt and seasoned the news to his own taste.

Annaise had fulfilled the mission with which Manuel had entrusted her. She had been from hut to hut to talk with the womenfolks. Some had proved obstinate. But the greater number, with sighs and "Ah, Lord! Good Lord!" had begun to figure out the change and the profit that irrigation would bring, and how much corn the fields would produce, how much millet and provisions and what price they would bring at the market. And I really need a few yards of cloth for a dress, and my man needs a pair of pants and a jacket. As for the children, there's no use talking about them, they're living almost naked, and it's a sin and a shame—all the more so since, in spite of poverty and disease, they are shooting up fast like bad weeds. (It's hard to kill a Negro off. He's tough like nobody's business!)

Nobody knew what the men thought about it. Some had assembled at Larivoire's hut. He was an old man, noted for his good counsel. Furthermore, someone had seen his son, Similien, coming out of Florentine's with a bottle of *clairin*, for it's a known fact, *clairin* makes the tongue light and ideas more supple.

Antoine had come to Bienaimé's, hobbling as fast as he could. He was beaming. He had but one word, *coumbite*, on his lips. He claimed that he would compose a song about Manuel, and that never in man's memory had he heard a more beautiful or a more work-stimulating theme.

But Bienaimé had cursed him out. That hadn't spoiled Antoine's good humor, though. Right now, sitting in front of his door, he was tightening the cords of his drum to give it the proper tension, so that the sounds would carry through distance and buzz the news to all the plain that a good life was beginning again.

"Well, Simidor," he said to himself, "let's see if you aren't rusty. Let's see if your fingers haven't gotten stiff. Let's see if your head is still as full of songs as a beehive is of honey."

He tried the drum, bent his ear down to it, and his toothless mouth stretched wide with laughter. Soon, in the rising sun, with his drum over his shoulder, he would be leading the peasants.

Already words began to graft themselves into the rhythm of a newborn melody:

> *General Manuel!*
> *Salute! Ho!*
> *Salute! Ho!*

His voice directed the rising and falling of the hoes:

Salute! Ho!
Salute! Ho!

Children ran up to listen. They crowded around him, but he chased the little Negroes away. He wanted to be alone so that nothing would disturb him while the song ripened in the beat of his drum.

Chapter Eleven

MANUEL BEGAN TO TALK to the peasants, one after the other. For years, hate had become with them a habit. It had given an object and a target to their impotent anger against the elements. But Manuel had translated into good Creole the exacting language of the thirsty plain, the plaint of growing things, the promises and all the mirages of the water. He had led them in advance through their harvest. Their eyes gleamed just from listening to him. Only there was one condition: that was reconciliation. And what did it cost them? A mere gesture, a few steps like walking over a bridge, and they would leave behind the bad days of poverty, they would enter the land of abundance.

"Well, brother, what do you say?"

The other, his feet bare in the dust, ragged, skinny, and famished, listened in silence. It was true that they were tired of that old story. What good was it, after all? Suppose they had a mass sung at the same time for both Dorisca and Sauveur, for the repose of their souls? That would reconcile them in the grave, then they'd leave the living in peace. Restless dead folks are troublesome, they're even dangerous. What was sure and certain was that we mustn't let ourselves perish. Well?

"Well, since it's like that, we agree. But who'll go and talk with the others?"

"I will," Manuel replied.

The others had met at Larivoire's. The news was serious. It merited deliberation. Larivoire stroked the scant hairs of his goatee. His eyes were calm and shrewd, his mouth prudent. What he saw, he measured. What he said, he had first weighed pro and con. His great age had taught him such wisdom. In the bloody feud that divided Fonds Rouge, he had taken sides only because of family ties. But he had done so with moderation, taking care not to excite folks, even appeasing them when the need arose. His word was heeded and respected. His opinion had the weight of a judge's sentence.

"So they're going to have water," Mauléon began.

He said no more. His glance went over the main road, toward his fields beaten down by sunlight. He owed fifteen *gourdes* to Florentine. Hilarion was demanding his bay mare in payment for these debts. A good animal and worth four times that much! And Cia, his wife, down with that fever that was wasting her away and which no medicine had been able to check. Dorméus claimed that an evildoer had cast a spell on her, so he was asking a large sum of money to rid her of it. The greedy dog! *Oui,* they had their share of trouble, for that they could vouch!

The sun shone through the palm leaves which covered the arbor, and drew a striped mat on the ground. A bottle of white rum and some enameled cups were placed on the rough-hewn table. Pierrilis helped himself, poured a few drops on the ground, then swallowed the rest at one gulp.

"Who knows if it's true?" he asked. He wiped his mouth with the back of his hand. "Yes," he repeated, "it remains to be seen if the news is true."

Larivoire slid back his chair, propping it against one of the poles in the arbor. He squinted his eyes. On the savanna, the light was doing a dance of white-hot needles. It was unbearable.

"A lie," he said, "is like money loaned out. It's got to bring in a profit. What interest would this Manuel have in lying? What profit would he get from it?"

"Well, they'd be able to water their fields," sighed Termonfils.

"And we'd hang around watching them, dry-mouthed," said Ismael.

Crouched on his heels, Gervilen said nothing. His small eyes, buried under the protection of his eyebrows, were nursing a disturbing fire.

"They're lucky, damn them!" Josaphat muttered.

He had just set up housekeeping with a young girl from Mahotière. For two days they had lived on nothing but crackers sopped in a little syrup. She didn't complain, Marianna, but she was silent as a shadow. That was worse than any reproach.

"No!" Nérestan exclaimed. He brought his fist down on the table with all his might. "I say no!" His thick chest was panting. Sweat bathed his face.

"No, what?" Larivoire asked, pulling on the hair of his beard.

Nérestan sat down again. Speaking had never come easily to him. That was why he was as violent as a wild bull. What he couldn't explain in words, he put under your nose with his fist. His hands were like washing paddles, capable of turning a man blue without dye.

There was silence. Larivoire's gamecock beat his cinnamon-colored wings and crowed. Other cocks answered him from the depths of neighboring courtyards.

"I'd rather leave Fonds Rouge," Josaphat said, "than stay here and watch them enjoy life while the rest of us feed on misery."

"So you're going to take to the highway and beg for alms from door to door?" Louisimé Jean-Pierre sneered.

"My fields used to produce thirty bags of corn, full measure," Ismael said. "As for sweet potatoes, there were enough to fatten the hogs. The earth's still there—good earth waiting only for a little water. How many seasons since the rain fell, I wonder? How long?"

"All that's idle talk," Mauléon interrupted. "What are we going to do?"

"There's nothing *to* do," said Josaphat, shrugging his shoulders hopelessly.

"Are you men or dogs?" Gervilen bounded to his feet, shaking with rage. His eyes were darting sparks in his charcoal face. A bit of froth whitened his mouth. "Sitting there like old women telling a rosary about their poverty! Not one brave Negro in the lot of you!" He spat scornfully. "Bunch of capons!"

Nérestan stood up. He was a head taller than Gervilen. "You haven't the right, no, you haven't the right," he stammered.

"Sit down!" Gervilen snapped. To everyone's amazement, Nérestan obeyed. He swayed on his chair like a bear, his head sunk on his shoulders.

"I tell you what we're going to do." Gervilen's voice was harsh now and grating like a rake. The words passed with difficulty through his clenched teeth. "We'll take the water! We'll take it by force!"

"That's the way to talk, boy!" Nérestan exulted. Tumult arose. Each one wanted to be heard. Women came out to their gates to see what was happening.

Larivoire raised his arms. "I'm speaking," he said. He waited for the uproar to subside. "I'm speaking, and you'll do well to listen to me if you want to avoid misfortune. You, Gervilen, from the dead Dorisca you've inherited blood that's too hot. I'm not saying that to reproach you. Even as a little tyke, you showed that character. Sister Miramise, your mama, should have whipped you—but no monkey ever thinks her baby's ugly, if I may say so without offending you. You speak of taking the water by force, but only the law has the right of force. You'll all wind up in jail. There's some more news that's important, too. Annaise came to see my wife no later than this morning."

At the mention of Annaise, Gervilen's whole body shook and his features froze as if cut in black rock.

"So Annaise came and, according to what she's heard, it seems there'd have to be a *coumbite* of all the peasants of Fonds Rouge if we are to bring the water to the plain, because it's a hard job—a task too difficult for Manuel's side to accomplish all by itself. Therefore, if we don't make up, the water will have to stay where it is."

Gervilen burst out laughing. His laugh was frightful to hear. It was like tearing a sheet of rusty tin.

"Can't you see," he shouted, "that Manuel and Annaise are in cahoots?"

"Be careful!" cautioned Gille. "You're talking about my sister."

"Shut your trap, imbecile!" Gervilen howled.

"Now, cousin," Gille said in a slow, drowsy tone. His hand quickly seized the handle of his machete.

"Are you both crazy?" Larivoire had rushed between them. "Negroes with no decency. Ah, accursed Negroes! So you want to shed blood in my house with no regard for my white hair!"

"Excuse me," said Gille, "but he insulted my sister."

"I told the truth," Gervilen retorted, "and if the truth tastes like blood, let it! I say let it! Let it!"

"You, Gervilen, get over there! Gille, sit here!" Larivoire ordered. He turned to the peasants. "Your ears have heard. What do you say?"

"Brothers!" Gervilen shouted. "They're trying to buy you. They're trying to trade your honor for a little water."

"Be quiet!" Larivoire said. "Let somebody else talk."

But the peasants were silent. They felt Gervilen's stare on their faces, eating its way into the depth of their thoughts.

Water! Its sunlit path across the plain. Its splash in the garden canal. Its ripple when it meets tufts of plants along its course. The soft reflection of the sky mixed with the fleeting image of the reeds. Black girls filling their dripping calabashes and their red clay pitchers at the spring. The chant of the washerwomen. The fertile soil. The tall ripening crops. They were struggling with temptation.

"We need to think about that," Ismael murmured.

"Some Negroes have no shame—just like dogs!" said Gervilen bitterly.

Ismael didn't answer. "Thirty bags of corn," he was thinking, "and sweet potatoes and victuals."

The other peasants were also reckoning the possible yield of their fields, making plans, anticipating the future. But they didn't dare say anything. Gervilen's presence disturbed them. He was camped in their midst, and his gaze went like a furious rat from one to the other.

Larivoire understood their hesitation. "Good! There's no hurry. On the contrary, we've got to look at this thing with a clear head. Tomorrow, if-God-wills, we'll meet and make a decision."

The peasants got up. Savagely, Gervilen left first without saying goodbye to anyone, not even Larivoire. At the gate, Nérestan joined him and, in that humble tone that giants take when they speak to little men who dominate them, "Brother Gervilen, I've something to say to you."

"Excrement!" the other replied, without even turning around.

Chapter Twelve

BIENAIMÉ REMAINED DIFFICULT. He hardly addressed a word to Manuel except to order, "Do this! Do that! Bring me the spotted heifer. I'm going to sell her myself at Pont Beudet."

Through Annaise, Manuel had learned what had taken place at Larivoire's. Gille had gone home choked with anger and talking about nothing except to cut off Gervilen's head to the root to cure him of his insolence. Fat Rosanna, who could already see her son in the hands of the police, had had a stroke. She had lost consciousness. This had frightened Gille terribly, and at the same time had calmed him down. But he declared himself in favor of reconciliation. He set out on a campaign to persuade the others, especially the younger ones, and he succeeded more or less in winning over Mauléon, Ismael, Termonfils, and Pierrilis.

Larivoire encouraged them on the sly. Only Gervilen and Nérestan were against them. Others were still hesitating, but more and more feebly, for what Manuel had foreseen had happened—the womenfolks had begun to make life impossible for them. They nagged their men mercilessly, buzzing about their ears with a thousand questions and innumerable complaints. They were worse than wasps. In vain the men would escape them to catch a breath of air or gulp down a grog at Florentine's place. On their return, the women would be waiting at the gate or on the doorstep, and the recriminations would start all over again with renewed vigor.

Louisimé Jean-Pierre had lost his temper and had even lifted his hand to impose silence on his unleashed *Négresse* with a good clout, but the latter had threatened to yell, "Murder!" For fear of scandal, Louisimé had abstained—

which had left the hollow of his hand itching. The woman, seeing herself triumphant, had began to vex him with all kinds of proverbs like, "Rotten teeth are strong only on rotten bananas"—which meant that he was treating her thus only because she was a weak defenseless woman. She had continued in this vein for a good while, and in the end, Louisimé, who hadn't been able to restrain himself, slapped her right on her talking machine. Then, instead of arousing the neighborhood, she had burst into tears, which softened Louisimé's heart and made him ashamed and sorry.

Even Marianna, Josaphat's wife, had found her tongue.

"At Mahotière," she was saying, "they've got water, and irrigation isn't even necessary for their fields. The cool morning dew suffices. At dawn, all is shiny and moist. You should see it. It's like foam from the sun." She sighed, "*Oui, mes amis*, life is easy at Mahotière, thank God, *oui*."

Josaphat asked her, "What do you think about this reconciliation business?"

"You are the masters, you men. It's up to you to decide."

They were in their hut. He drew her to him, his pretty young sweetheart. He pressed her in his arms.

"Josaphat, my man," she said, "I've been wanting to tell you this for several days. I'm going to have a baby, dear. But I'll never be strong enough to bear this baby if we keep on living in such misery."

Josaphat released her, his brow contracted. "You really believe that . . . ?

"Yes," she said firmly.

He seemed to think it over, then his face lighted up. "He's the one who's giving the orders, that little black baby! I'm going to tell Gille yes."

"It's life that's giving the orders," Marianna said, "and water that's life's answer!"

Thus things seemed to be working out satisfactorily and along the right road. Gervilen realized this only too well, and cursed right and left. Besides, since the meeting at Larivoire's, he hadn't once stopped drinking. Nérestan kept him company. But, quite the reverse of Gervilen, *tafia* disposed Nérestan to see the agreeable side of life. None of his violence remained. He became as easily handled as a barrel. One had but to push him down the slope and he'd roll to the depths of blessed intoxication. Gervilen had tried to excite him. Nothing doing. Nérestan would open his enormous mouth and laugh. About what? About a story he'd heard a long time ago. He had forgotten it but he was sure it had been funny. In the end, Gervilen had insulted him, and Nérestan had gone off irritated, bending under the influence of his grog, like the mast of a sailboat in a heavy storm, and telling everyone he met that nothing but his good nature had kept him, Nérestan, from squashing Gervilen like a flea.

Naturally, the whole story had reached Hilarion's ears. It didn't please him, not at all. This Manuel fellow was damn well upsetting his plans. If the peasants succeeded in watering their land, they'd refuse to yield it in payment of the debts and loans at usurious rates that they were piling up at his Florentine's. He'd have to lock Manuel up in the town jail, and make him tell where the spring was located. They had ways of making folks talk.

Then he'd leave the peasants to dry off in expectation, and when they had lost courage and all hope, he, Hilarion, would seize their fields and become the owner of several fine, well irrigated plots of land. The rub was that he'd have to split it with the lieutenant and the justice of the peace. They were greedy! But Hilarion would arrange to keep the lion's share. The first thing to do was get hold of Manuel. Besides, he was a bad character, a dangerous Negro, who spoke words of rebellion to the peasants.

"You'll only be doing your duty," Florentine told him. She was a former prostitute from Croix des Bouquets whom Hilarion had picked up out of the gutter, and whose thirst for money devoured her like a malignant fever. "This Manuel is against established law and order. He's against the Government."

"My hand on my conscience," Hilarion swore. With a broad hairy paw he covered the rural policeman's badge that shone on his chest. "My hand on my conscience, in God's truth, that's my duty!"

Who could say that life was soon to have a rebirth at Fonds Rouge?

In the flaming afternoon the mountain stood erect, its sides bled white by rock gullies. The breadfruit trees, sick from the drought, served as a perch for crows. When their vehement cawing slackened for a second, you could hear the breathless cry of guinea hens in the thorn acacias. A hot decomposed odor, that the wind beat down on the village along with swarms of mosquitoes, rose from Zombi Pool.

"Is it on good and tight?" Bienaimé asked.

"Yes," Manuel answered, pulling one last time at the strap.

Délira lifted her head toward the sun. "You'll get there before nightfall." She sighed. She had done her best to discourage him from undertaking this trip.

The bandy-legged chestnut horse that Dorismond had loaned them for the occasion was waiting under the calabash tree. Bienaimé put his foot in the stirrup and pulled himself up on the saddle with some difficulty. This saddle was the last splendor that he had left, but the saddleblanket was missing. A sack replaced it.

"*Adieu*, Délira," Bienaimé said. And to Manuel, "Untie the animal. Give me the rope. Go and open the gate."

"*Adieu*, my man," said Délira.

Bienaimé clicked his tongue and spurred the chestnut horse with a kick of his heels. The heifer followed docilely. Manuel had removed the thick bamboo poles that served as a gate.

"Have a good trip, *oui*, papa," he said.

"Thanks," Bienaimé replied dryly, without looking at him.

Manuel went back toward the house. The lizards were dragging their soft, fat bellies through the dust of the path, or scooting off to chase one another under the hedge of the chandelier trees in the thistle-covered garden.

"For a stubborn man, you can't beat him!" the old woman complained. "As if you couldn't have managed that sale in his stead. Can it be that he doesn't realize how old he is? Now he's going to have to spend the night at Beudet on some porch or other, and in the cool night air. That's no good for his rheumatism. Not to mention the fact that he'll have to come back over that same long route tomorrow afternoon. That Bienaimé's certainly one hardheaded Negro!"

Although Manuel had tried to spare his father the fatigue of this trip, he hadn't insisted very much to get him to give it up. He wanted to take advantage of his absence to go to the meeting that would take place that evening at Larivoire's. He wanted to surprise the peasants by his unexpected presence, give them no time to change their mind, and convince them that there was no other solution to their problem save reconciliation. To occupy his impatience, he began to weave a macaw hat. His mother sat near him on the porch.

"Early this morning," she said, "I met Annaise. She must have been going to Mahotière to do the washing, for she was carrying a basket filled with clothes. She said, '*Bonjour, bonjour*, mama!' That's what she said to me."

Manuel's diligent fingers laced and interlaced the straw.

"And you know how I answered her? '*Bonjour*, daughter-in-law!' That's how I answered her. She showed me her teeth in a smile. She's got what I call beautiful white teeth, big eyes, black skin, smooth as silk, and, furthermore, she's a long-haired *Négresse*. I saw one of her curls dangling out from her madras. In truth, the Good Lord has adorned her with His own hands!

"But, you see, what really matters isn't so much a pretty face, but good manners, and Annaise seems quite proper, I can't deny that. These days, that isn't very easy to find, no. There are too many of these young girls who've lost their respect for the ways of our ancestors. The city has turned their heads. You might say the soles of their feet have been rubbed with pepper. They can't stand still, the shameless hussies! The land is no longer good enough for them. They'd rather go to work as cooks for some rich mulattoes. As if that was the thing to do!"

The old woman made a wry, contemptuous face. "A sin, I say it's a sin, that's what I say."

Brother, you don't know the spring at Mahotière? Then you're not from around here, brother. Between the legs of the mountain that spring flows. You leave the huts and the fields and by the ease of the slope you reach the ravine. It's a cool ravine because of the steep cliffs and the branches of the *mombin* trees that shade it. Ferns are everywhere in its oozing humidity, and a mat of watercress and mint wades in its cooling current. Under the rocks you catch crayfish, not very big ones, for they're the color of sunlit water so that they can't be seen very easily, the sly rascals! Still you can catch them by the basketful. And with rice it's a very good dish, take my word for it.

The sun delights in playing on the pebbles, and the water makes an incessant babble which mingles with the washerwomen's paddles on the wet clothes. That creates a never-failing din, a laughing music that accompanies the chant of the *Négresses*.

No, they're not to be pitied, the Mahotière folk. They have everything they need, what with their rich red soil built up in terraces, good for all crops. Avocado and mango trees protect their huts from the heat of day, and on their fences you can see those bunches of tiny, rosy bells—what do they call those flowers? 'Pretty Mexican Maids,' that's what they call them.

But the peasants' luckiest possession is that spring. There isn't any better or clearer drinking water anywhere around. And over by Plaisance, in the open curve of the ravine, it reaches the flat of the plain which the Negroes of the region have laid out for their ricefields.

The old folks of Mahotière will tell you that the Mistress of the Water is a mulatto woman. At midnight she comes out of the spring singing, combing her long, dripping hair which makes a music sweeter than violins. It's a song of perdition for anyone who hears it. There's no sign of the cross or, "In the name of the Father," that can save him. Its evil charm catches him like a fish in a net and the Mistress of the Water waits for him at the edge of the spring and sings and smiles at him, and beckons for him to follow her down into the bottomless water from whence he will never return.

Annaise had spread out her clothes to dry on the pebbles: her dresses, her blue, violet, and red bandannas, all her things. Her brother Gille's pants with wide patches where it would be shameful for them not to be, Rosanna's lace-flounced skirts such as elderly women wear, and the white kerchiefs that must be well starched because her mother wore them on her head with her black shawl when she went into town.

She bent over the wash. Her busy hands twisted the clothes and made the soap squirt. She looked like some queen of Guinea with her curved hips, her naked breasts, hard and pointed, her skin so black and smooth.

Her cousin, Roselia, did her washing beside her. She talked continually, relating Fonds Rouge stories, those that were true and those she invented. She had a sharp tongue, that Roselia. But Annaise heard her without listening. Her thoughts were with Manuel.

Manuel, dear, she thought, and a warm wave swept over her, a weakness so sweet that she wanted to close her eyes as she had done last night when he kissed her and she had felt herself drifting in a burning current whose every wave was a thrill to her body. He had covered her completely, he had become one with her, and she had left his mouth only long enough to emit that lacerating cry of the blood that gushed from the depths of her flesh and flowered into a happy sigh of deliverance.

I'm his woman, she dreamt, and she smiled. You had to come all the way back from Cuba to find me here. It's a story that begins like a fairy tale, "Once upon a time." But it's a tale that ends happily, "I'm your wife!" Because, oh, God! some are full of death and disaster.

"You're not working any more. Are you tired?" Roselia asked.

Annaise shook her head as though coming out of a dream. "No, cousin," she said. She seized her paddle and pounded her clothes. The indigo faded in the stream to blend with the current.

Roselia already had four children. Her bosom was dry and flabby. She looked enviously at Annaise's well-filled breasts, with nipples mauve as grapes.

"You ought to get married," she remarked.

"I?" said Annaise. "I've plenty of time ahead of me." She choked back a little laugh that the other mistakenly took for the timidity of a young *Négresse*. But it was a laugh that meant, "How surprised you'll be when you see me in my hut with my husband, Manuel, and there'll be bay trees in our garden and reeds by our canal."

The day ended in dusk, the sky darkened, the mountain disappeared, the woods entered the shadow, a thin slice of moon began its trip through the clouds, and night came.

One after the other, the kitchen fires had been extinguished. You could hear the voice of some irritated woman calling her little black son who, for some reason, had tarried in the yard despite his great fear of the werewolf. A dog howled, a second answered him, and, from door to door, a concert of barking got under way. The time to rest had arrived, when everyone went to stretch out on his pallet, close his eyes, and try to forget his troubles in sleep.

Fonds Rouge slumbered in the black night. There wasn't a light, except at Larivoire's, where a candle stood in the middle of the table under the arbor. Several peasants were already there with the master of the hut, his son Similien, Gille, Josaphat, Ismael, Louisimé. The others would come soon. Manuel knew, so he waited.

"Tell me, Manuel, are you asleep, Manuel?" his mother called from the next room.

Sitting on the bed, he didn't answer. He pretended to be asleep. Before the picture of a saint, with its wick soaked in castor oil, the eternal lamp burned dimly. A breath of air entered through the ill-fitting window flap, stirred the flame, and brightened its faded colors. It was a picture of St. James there, who is at the same time Ogoun, the Dahomey god. He had a fierce air, with his bristly beard, his brandished saber. As the flame licked the dappled red of his clothing, it looked like fresh blood.

In the silence, Manuel heard his mother turn over on her straw mat, seeking the right place to sleep. She was whispering words he couldn't understand, a prayer, perhaps, one last prayer. Délira was a person who called angels by their first names.

Time passed. Manuel finally became impatient. He went to the door and listened. "Mama," he called softly. He heard her peaceful breathing. The old woman had fallen asleep.

Manuel opened the window very cautiously. The rusty hinges scraped a bit. He slipped out into the night. The little dog recognized him without barking, and trotted along at his heels for a moment. It was dark as the devil. Fortunately, a thin thread of moonlight ran along the path. The chandelier trees raised a wall of shadows about the garden. Crickets chirped in the grass. Manuel stepped over the fence. He found himself on the main road.

It wasn't far to Larivoire's hut. The light beckoned to him and guided him. He passed Annaise's place.

Bonsoir, sweet *Négresse*, he thought.

He imagined her sleeping, her face on her curved arm, and a passionate longing for her came over him. This week, Bienaimé and Délira would carry the proposal letter to Rosanna. What lovely words *Monsieur* Paulma had written! He had read them aloud for Manuel, licking his lips in contentment, as if syrup were flowing from his mouth. And then he had offered him some rum, an exquisite rum, in truth.

He had always regretted, Manuel had, not knowing how to write. But when, thanks to irrigation, existence became easier, they'd ask the Communal Magistrate in town to set up a school in Fonds Rouge. Manuel would propose that the peasants, of their own volition, build a hut to house it. Instruction was a necessary thing; it helped you understand life.

Take, for example, that comrade in Cuba, who talked with him about politics at the time of the strike. He knew things, that *hijo de su madre*! And he could explain the most intricate problems ever so clearly. You could see each question strung up before you on the cord of his reasoning like rinsed clothes hung out to dry in the sun. He would explain the thing so plainly that you could grab it with your hand like a piece of good bread. He put it, so to speak, within your reach. And if a peasant went to school, surely it wouldn't be so easy any more to cheat him, abuse him, and treat him like a beast of burden.

He reached Larivoire's gate. Night shrouded him. The peasants were in a circle under the arbor. Gervilen was speaking, the others listened. Larivoire was shaking his head, trying to interrupt, but Gervilen continued, flaying the air with his arms and stamping his feet.

"Honor," Manuel cried.

"Respect," Larivoire replied.

Manuel advanced rapidly. The peasants recognized him as he came into the light. Some got up. Others remained nailed to their chairs, gaping, petrified with amazement.

"I've come, brothers," Manuel said.

"Enter with respect," Larivoire answered.

"I bid you good evening, brothers."

There were some who replied reluctantly, others, not at all. Larivoire offered his chair.

"With your permission," Manuel said, "I'll remain standing before your white hair."

Larivoire smiled with the corners of his lips. Manuel knows manners, he does. Manuel leaned his shoulder against a pole.

"I've come with peace and reconciliation."

"Speak," Larivoire said. "We're listening."

"It's true, *oui*, what they're saying. I swear it on the head of my old mother—I've discovered a big spring."

"Lies!" Nérestan growled.

"I've taken an oath, Brother Nérestan, and I'm not accustomed to lying. Remember when we were young fellows, no bigger than that, you were accused one day of stealing some ears of corn from Dorismond's garden. And I stepped up and confessed, although I knew my papa'd tear the skin off my back with his whip."

"That's true!" Nérestan exclaimed. "I'll say, you've got a good memory!" He was laughing now with his whole enormous mouth, and pounding his thighs with blows hard enough to knock off a Christian's head.

"Close your teeth!" Gervilen snapped angrily.

"Those ears of corn, I had stolen to roast in the woods

with Josaphat and Pierrilis. In those days we used to share things."

He's a clever Negro! Larivoire reflected, admiringly. He's warded off the storm.

"I left for foreign lands," Manuel continued, "and when I returned, I found Fonds Rouge pillaged by drought and plunged into the deepest kind of poverty." He waited a moment. "And I found the peasants divided up and quarreling."

The trouble was starting again. The peasants' faces contracted. Manuel went straight to his objective. "There's only one way to escape from drought and misery—that is to end this feud."

"We can't ever end blood," Gervilen cried. "Blood has flowed, Dorisca's blood. He was my father. You've forgotten?"

"But Sauveur died in prison," Larivoire countered. "Vengeance was gotten."

"No, for I wasn't the one to kill him with these hands, with my own hands!" A frenzied grimace twisted Gervilen's face. He was waving his hands like enormous spiders.

"Brother Gervilen," Manuel began.

"Don't call me brother. I'm nothing to you."

"All peasants are equals," Manuel said. "They're all one single family. That's why they call each other 'brother,' 'cousin,' 'brother-in-law.' One needs the other. One perishes without the other's help. That's the lesson of the *coumbite*. This spring that I've found needs the help of all the peasants of Fonds Rouge. Don't say no. It's life that gives orders. When life commands, we've got to answer, 'Present!' "

"Well spoken!" Gille approved.

"Life's giving the orders!" Wasn't that exactly what Marianna had said? Josaphat stood up. "Present!" he said, "I agree."

"Tell me, is there *enough* water?" Ismael asked. "Because my fields once yielded thirty sacks of corn, full measure."

"Everyone will have enough for his needs and his crops."

"You putrid bastard!" Gervilen spat, turning so brutally toward Ismael that the latter gripped his machete.

"Ah, Brother Gervilen!" he said, slowly shaking his head, but keeping his eyes vigilant. "You're not careful with your tongue. You lack respect for your equals. You'll regret that some day, *oui!*"

"A dirty lowdown Negro if ever there was one!" Mauléon muttered.

"I see, you're all against me." Gervilen spoke as if he were tasting sticky bile. "You've sold your honor for a few drops of water."

"You'd sell yours, all right, for white rum."

Gervilen pretended not to have heard Gille. "As for you, Larivoire, you've defended the family well. Thanks, I say, thanks—because, out of respect for your age, I can't tell you what I think of you as I can tell this bunch of swine!"

"But," Larivoire objected impatiently, "can't you think a moment? Can't you let some sense into your head?"

"No, damn it! I don't want to." He walked toward Manuel, and stopped two paces away from him. He stared at him for a long time, as though he were taking his measurements, then said with a smile that tore his mouth, "You've crossed the path of Gervilen Gervilis twice. Once was already too much!" Then he disappeared in the night.

The peasants felt relieved after his departure. They breathed more at ease.

"I guess an evil spirit is tormenting him," said Louisimé Jean-Pierre.

"He's a nuisance, that Negro," Pierrilis added.

Manuel hadn't budged from his place. He brushed Gervilen from his thoughts as one waves away a mosquito. He was awaiting the peasants' decision.

Naturally, they agreed, the peasants did, but they couldn't reply like that on the double-quick. That would make them seem too anxious. After all, this Manuel mustn't think that he had carried the day so easily. They had their dignity, didn't they?

Being clever, Larivoire understood the turn things were taking. "You came honorably, and we've listened to you. But it's too early yet to say yes or no. Wait till tomorrow, if-it's-God's-will. I'll bring you the answer myself."

"I'm already in favor," said Gille.

"I answered 'present,' " Josaphat added.

"I'm not against it," said Pierrilis.

"Me either," Ismael chimed in.

But the others kept silent.

"You see," Larivoire concluded, "there are some who haven't yet decided. Let me say, without wishing to put you out, we have to examine the matter among ourselves. Thanks for your visit, brother."

"You've said a word that's agreeable to hear, Larivoire. I, too, give you my thanks, brother peasants. And if that Gervilen returns, tell him, please, that I bear him no hard feelings, that here is my hand. And that it's a hand wide open for peace and reconciliation."

Nérestan got up. He walked heavily toward Manuel. His head almost touched the roof of the arbor. His shoulders blocked the view of four peasants.

What a woodsman it would take to notch and fell a man like that! Manuel reflected on seeing him approach.

"Brother Manuel," Nérestan said, "I'd forgotten that story about the corn. This Negro's no ingrate. Thank God, Nestor Nérestan's no ingrate!"

He offered his gigantic hand. Manuel took it. Terrific strength slept in those thick fingers, rough as bark.

"Salut!" said Manuel.

"Salut!" Nérestan repeated.

In a single gesture, each touched his forehead with his hand.

"At your service," said Nérestan.

"At your service," Manuel repeated.

Larivoire tapped him on the shoulder. "*Adieu*, son, you're a good man. You'll see me tomorrow afternoon."

"Well, *adieu*, Larivoire," Manuel replied.

"Take this piece of pine wood. It'll light your way." Larivoire tendered him a lighted torch whose flame went up in smoke and spread an odor of resin.

"You're very polite," Manuel thanked him. "Well, cousins, *adieu, oui.*"

This time, they all responded. Their voices no longer hesitated. They sounded a note of friendship.

Manuel passed through the gate. He was now on the main road. The pine torch cast a bit of light about him. A piece of fence protruded in the shadow. A surprised pig, hiding in the thistles, ran off snorting. Manuel walked with a light heart. What a garden of stars in the sky! And the moon crept among them so brilliant and sharp that the stars should have fallen like cut flowers.

I'm sure that Larivoire will bring the right answer tomorrow. You've done your duty, you've fulfilled your mission, Manuel. Life's going to start all over in Fonds Rouge, and now you can build that hut. Three doors will it have, I repeat, two windows, a porch with a railing, and a little stoop. The corn will grow so high that the hut can't be seen from the road.

He was walking past Annaise's hedge of chandelier trees. That's how it'll be, my sweet *Négresse*. You'll see your man's no idler, but a strong fellow up each day at the first crow of the rooster, a hard-working tiller of the land, a real Master of the Dew!

Back in the yard under the trees her hut was asleep. He stopped a moment. He inhaled the odor of logwood blossoms, and a great, deep, calm joy penetrated his being.

Rest, Anna darling, rest until the rising of the sun.

A crackle of crushed grass made him turn around. He had no time to parry the blow. A shadow danced before him, then struck again. The taste of blood rose in his mouth. He staggered and fell.

His torch went out.

Chapter Thirteen

HE REGAINED CONSCIOUSNESS, and the light of the distant stars wavered slowly and dizzily. A sharp pain nailed him to the ground.

"That scoundrel! I'm going to die!"

He tried to get up, but fell back on his face. "I'm going to die in the road like a dog."

He succeeded in raising up on his elbows to drag himself a little way. He was too weak to cry for help. Who would have heard him in this night given over to silence and to sleep?

With a tremendous effort, his side and shoulder pierced by dagger thrusts, he rose, staggering like a drunken man. His knees trembled, his feet were like lead. And still, that rolling sky, that awful nausea! He reeled a few steps forward. Each step thrust terrible pain through his wounds. He wiped his mouth where the blood flowed.

With his hands outstretched like a blind man feeling his way through the darkness, he crossed the road, but his foot slipped in the ditch and he fell. Clawing at the thistles and weeds with his fingernails, he crawled to the fence, and stood up again in an effort of desperate determination. He was panting and an icy sweat moistened his face. His clutching fingers followed the fence. He moved in a night filled with flashes of light, his head dangling as he stumbled against the stones. Sick fainting spells, when he vomited something thick, something clotted, made his legs buckle. With his arm he caught hold of a post, but his weight pulled him down and he rolled to the ground.

He revived weaker each time. But the unbreakable resolve to reach the gate of his own hut renewed his flagging strength. He went forward on his belly and pulled himself up to the fence. The sky had paled, and in the east, a fringe of light heralded the dawn as he achieved his gate. He crawled under the bamboo pole. The path wavered before him like a stream in the moonlight. The little dog ran up to him, barking in distress, frightened by this man crawling on his hands and knees toward the door.

He fell against the door with his whole body.

"Who's there?" the old woman cried.

"Mama!" he groaned.

The dog howled.

"I say, 'Who's there?' " the old woman repeated.

She got up to light the lamp. A mortal anguish made her tremble.

Outside the door, in the dark, a broken moan, "Please, mama, quick!"

"Manuel? Jesus-Mary-Joseph!"

He lay stretched out before her. With her frail arms she pulled his huge body into the house. Then she saw the blood and screamed.

"I knew it! I knew it! They've murdered him! They've killed my boy! Help, friends! Help, neighbors!"

"Quiet, mama, quiet!" said Manuel in a low breath. "Close the door and help me to bed, mama."

She almost carried him to the bed. Where did she get that strength, old Délira? The thought that he was about to die almost drove her out of her head. She undressed him. Two small black wounds pierced his side and his back. She tore a sheet, bandaged the wounds, and went to light the fire to boil some calabash leaves.

Manuel lay there, his eyes closed, hardly breathing. The eternal lamp burned under Ogoun's picture. The god was brandishing his saber and his crimson cloak wrapped him in a cloud of blood.

Blinded by tears, Délira sat down beside him. Manuel's lips moved.

"Mama, are you there, mama? Stay near me, mama."

"Yes, my little one. Yes, dear, I'm here." She kissed his hand, hugged his earth-soiled hand. "Tell me the scoundrel's name so I can send word to Hilarion."

He became agitated. "No! No!" his weakened voice pleaded. "That won't do any good. The water, we've got to save the water! The wood pigeons, they flap their wings in its foliage, the wood pigeons. Ask Annaise about the road that runs up to the great fig tree, the road to the water."

His haggard eyes were shining. She sponged his brow that was bathed in a heavy sweat. His chest seemed to be lifting a crushing weight. Little by little he grew calmer, then dozed off. Délira didn't dare leave him.

"My God, my saints, dear Virgin, my angels! Please, please, oh, please make him live! Because if he dies, what will this old Délira do on earth? Tell me, what's she going to do on earth all alone, without consolation in her old age, with no reward for all this misery she's endured all her life? You, Mama of Jesus at the foot of the cross, oh, Virgin of the Miracles! I ask your forgiveness, forgiveness, mercy for my boy! Take me instead! I've lived my time, but he's still in the days of his youth, poor young devil! Let him live, do you hear, dear? Do you hear, Little Mama? My good dear Little Mama of Jesus, you hear me, don't you?"

Torn by a sob, she fell to her knees, arms outspread. She kissed the earth.

"Earth, Holy Earth, don't drink his blood! In the name of the Father, and of the Son, and of the Holy Ghost, Amen!"

She wept, she prayed. But what good are prayers and supplications when that last hour has come of which the Book speaks? When the moon goes out and the stars go out and the wax of the clouds hides the sun, and the strong Negro says, "I'm tired," and the *Négresse* stops pounding the corn because she's tired, and there's a bird laughing in the weeds like a rusty rattle, and those who sing are sitting in a circle without a word, and those who weep are running down the main street of the town and crying "Help! Help! Today we're burying our beloved, and he's going off toward the grave, he's going off toward the dust!"

The daylight slipped through the badly hung flap of the window. Some hens started cackling as usual. Manuel opened his eyes. He reached for the air with little panting gasps.

"You're awake, son?" Délira asked. "How do you feel? How does your body feel?"

He whispered, "Thirsty."

"Do you want a little coffee?"

He indicated yes by closing his eyelids. Délira went to heat the coffee and returned with the warm infusion of calabash leaves. She washed his wounds. Very little blood had flowed.

"I'm thirsty," he repeated.

The old woman brought the coffee. She held Manuel in her arms and he drank with difficulty. His head fell back on the pillow.

"Open the window, mama."

He looked at the patch of light that spread in the sky. He smiled feebly. "Day is breaking. Every day, day breaks. Life starts over again."

"Tell me, Manuel," Délira insisted, "tell me that bandit's name so I can send word to Hilarion."

His hands twisted nervously on the sheet. His fingernails were a scaly white. He spoke, but so softly that Délira was obliged to lean over him.

"Your hand, mama, your hand. Warm me. I feel so cold in my hands."

Délira gazed at him desperately. His eyes had grown quite wide in the depth of their sockets. A greenish circle lowered over his hollow cheeks.

He's going, she thought. My boy's going. Death is upon him.

"You hear me, mama?"

"I'm listening, *oui*, Manuel."

He collected his strength to speak. Through a haze of tears, Délira saw his breast heave and struggle.

"If you send word to Hilarion, then that old Sauveur-Dorisca story will start all over again—hate and revenge will live on among the peasants. The water will be lost. You've offered sacrifices to the *loas*. The blood of chickens and young goats you've offered to make the rain fall. That hasn't done any good—because what counts is the sacrifice of a man. The blood of a man. Go see Larivoire. Tell him the will of my blood that's been shed—reconciliation—reconciliation—so that life can start all over again, so that day can break on the dew."

Exhausted, he still whispered, "And sing my mourning, sing my mourning with a song of the *coumbite*."

"Honor!" cried a voice outside.

"Respect," Délira replied mechanically.

Hilarion's evil head framed itself in the window.

"Oh, *bonjour*, Délira."

"*Bonjour, oui.*"

He noticed the outstretched body.

"What's wrong with him? Sick?" His suspicious eyes squinted toward Manuel.

Délira hesitated, but she felt Manuel's hand pressing hers.

"Yes," she said, "he brought back some bad fevers from Cuba."

"Is he asleep?" Hilarion asked.

"He's asleep, *oui*."

"That's a shame, because the lieutenant wants him. He'll have to report at the barracks as soon as he can get up."

"All right, I'll tell him."

She listened to his steps move away, then she turned toward Manuel. A streamlet of black blood flowed from his mouth. His eyes were looking at her but he no longer saw her. He still held her hand. He had taken her promise with him.

Old Délira closed her boy's eyes. His bloodstained clothes she buried under the bed. Now she could wail the great cry of a wounded animal. Her neighbors heard it and the peasants came running, men and women. The news fell on their heads like a block of stone. They were crushed.

"Such a strong Negro! Only yesterday I was saying to Manuel, 'Brother Manuel . . .' It isn't natural, no, it isn't natural."

But Délira answered all their questions, "The fever, the bad fevers from that country of Cuba." And she uttered that awful cry, she opened her arms, and her old body trembled, crucified.

Laurélien arrived. He looked at the corpse. They lighted a candle at his head and another at his feet. There was a light on Manuel's forehead, and even in death his mouth kept that stubborn pucker.

"So, Chief? You've gone, Chief? You've gone?" Big tears rolled down his hard face.

"Ah, misery!" murmured Sister Destine.

"Ah, life!" Mérilia sighed.

"I'm waiting," the old woman repeated.

"Aunty," said Clairemise, "I'm going to help you bathe him."

But Déilra answered, "No, thanks . . . I'm waiting."

"You're waiting for whom, Aunty?"

Destine brought her a cup of tea. She refused. She swayed on her chair as though rocking her sorrow with her whole body. The others held her up and consoled her, but that was only talk. She didn't even hear them. She wailed as if claws of iron were mangling her soul.

Soon those others too had heard the news. They slipped into Larivoire's. Larivoire was seated under his arbor. He pulled on the hair of his beard. He did not answer their questions. Don't they know? Why, of course they know. Gervilen's door is closed, and he's not to be found anywhere.

The womenfolks met in front of their gates. "Now there's trouble for you," said one. And the other replied, "Yes, indeed."

As for Isménie, Louisimé Jean-Pierre's wife, she claimed that it was the vengeance of the Mistress of the Water. "That's what's dangerous, *oui*, sister, the spirit of the spring."

"But," her neighbor retorted, "they say this Manuel brought back the bad fevers from Cuba. They ate up his blood."

"They say, they say, what don't they say?" the incredulous ones remarked.

Hilarion sniffed the air like a dog looking for a trail. He scented a mystery. He sent his aide for information but everywhere mouths were stitched up tight. Or else folks acted as though they were completely surprised.

"So much the better!" Hilarion reflected. "That Manuel was a nuisance, a rebellious Negro. Now I can get the land from these peasant swine." That was also greedy Florentine's thought.

She for whom Délira was waiting came. Annaise was almost running, she had lost her senses. People could say what they wanted. What did she care? They'll know anyway. All right, let them know! Then what?

Manuel! Manuel! Oh, my brother! My sweetheart, darling! "You'll be the mistress of my hut," he said. "And there'll be reeds and bay trees in our garden...."

He had taken her by the spring where the sounds of the water had cut into her body like a fertile stream of life. Can a man die like that, as a breath of air blows out a candle, as a pruning knife cuts a weed, as fruit falls from a tree and rots, when he is such a big strong man? Now the crops would ripen—he wouldn't see them. The water would sing in the canal—he wouldn't hear it. And I, Annaise, your *Négresse*, I'll call you—but you won't answer me. No! No, God! It isn't true! It can't be! It wouldn't be right!

The peasants who saw her pass shook their heads. "*Mes amis*!" they marveled. "Has Rosanna's daughter lost her mind?"

When she entered the courtyard, they looked at her dumbfounded. Antoine, who was just arriving, stopped dead still with jaw unhinged. Jean-Jacques grumbled, "What does she want? The impertinent hussy!" And Sister Destine stepped forward, her fists on her hips, with a hostile gesture.

But Délira rose. She led Annaise by the hand. She took her in her arms and they wept together in great heartbroken sobs. Then everyone understood.

Clairemise, who had a good heart, murmured, "Poor girl, poor girl!"

Antoine said, "Life's a comedy, that's what life is!" He spat. "It's got a bitter taste, the bitch!"

Annaise knelt beside Manuel and took his already icy hand in hers. She called him, "Manuel, Manuel, ho!" in a gentle voice wet with tears. Then, with a savage cry, she fell back, her arms upraised, her face distorted.

"No, God, you're not good! It's not true that you're kind! It's a lie! We call on you to help us—you don't hear. Look at our grief! Look at our sorrow! Look at our tribulations! Are you asleep, God? Are you deaf? Are you blind? Have you got no heart, God? Where is your justice? Where is your pity? Where is your mercy?"

"Quiet, Annaise!" Délira ordered. "Sins come from your mouth."

But Annaise didn't hear her. "It's useless for poor Negroes to cry for grace and forgiveness. You crush us like millet under a mallet! You grind us up like dust! You bring us low! You knock us down! You destroy us!"

"Yes, brothers," sighed Antoine, "that's how it is! From Guinea to today the Negro's walked in storm and tempest and turmoil. 'The Good Lord's good,' they say. 'The Good Lord's white,' they *ought* to say. Or maybe it's just the reverse."

"Enough, Antoine! There're already enough curses on this hut."

Délira lifted Annaise to her feet "Get yourself together, daughter. We're going to bathe him."

The peasants left the room and Délira closed the door. She put her finger to her lips.

"Don't scream!"

Gently she turned the body over.

"Don't scream, I say!"

She lifted his shirt, and two small wounds, blacker than his skin, appeared, two little lips of clotted blood.

"Lord!" Annaise groaned.

Délira made the sign of the cross over the first wound.

"You've seen nothing."

She made the sign of the cross over the second wound.

"You know nothing."

She looked at Annaise sternly.

"It was his last wish. He was holding my hand and he went away bearing my promise. Swear that you'll keep this secret!"

"I swear, *oui*, mama."

"In the name of the Holy Virgin?"

"In the name of the Holy Virgin!"

It wasn't Manuel, that great, cold, stiff, lifeless body. It was only his likeness in stone. The real Manuel was walking through the mountains and the woods in the sunlight. He was talking to Annaise. "My darling," he was saying, taking her in his arms, enveloping her in his warmth. The real Manuel was making a canal so that the water might flow through the fields. He was walking in the harvests of the future, in the dew of early dawn.

"I haven't the courage, mama," Anna whispered, afraid.

"He was your man," the old woman said. "You've got to do your duty!"

Annaise lowered her head. "*Oui,* mama, I'll do my duty."

When the two women had completed their funereal task, when Manuel was dressed in his suit of coarse blue cloth, Délira relighted the candles.

"Put his machete by his side," she said. "He was a hard-working peasant."

Later in the afternoon, Bienaimé returned. He was bringing back the heifer that he hadn't been able to sell. The tired animal was limping again.

"What's this congregation in my yard?" he asked, perceiving a crowd of peasants. Laurélien opened the gate for him.

"I've got a son," said Bienaimé crossly, "and it has to be a neighbor who comes to open the gate for me. Thanks anyway, Laurélien."

He wanted to keep on toward the hut but Laurélien held back his horse by the bridle.

"Brother Bienaimé," he began.

At this moment, Délira came out of the hut. She advanced slowly, tall and thin in her black dress, her head wrapped in a white madras.

"Papa," she said, "get down from your horse and give me your hand."

"What's the matter?" the old man stuttered.

"Give me your hand, papa."

But her strength left her and she fell against Bienaimé's chest, shaken by bitter sobs.

In the hut the mourners' chorus started. The huge Destine was turning round and round, striking one hand against the other and screaming as if she had lost her mind.

"Ah, Lord! Good Lord! Here's Bienaimé, *mes amis,* here's Bienaimé!"

"Manuel?" said the old man in a toneless voice.

Délira clung to him in despair. "Yes, papa, yes! Bienaimé, dear papa, our boy! Our only son, the consolation of our old age."

The peasants moved aside as they passed. The women wailed.

"You don't have to invite misfortune in," Antoine opined. "It comes anyhow and sits at your table without permission. It eats and leaves nothing but bones."

Bienaimé looked at the corpse. He wasn't weeping, old Bienaimé wasn't. But the most hardened turned their eyes away from his face and coughed violently. Suddenly he tottered. The peasants rushed to him.

"Leave me alone," he said, pushing them away.

He went out of the hut. He sat down on a step in front of the porch, bent in two as if someone had broken his shoulders. His hands trembled in the dust.

The sun was about to set. Day had to end sometime. Angry clouds floated toward the horizon with all their sails aflame. In the savanna a herd of oxen took on a stone-like immobility. The hens already flapped their wings in the calabash trees.

Some peasants came as others left. They had to take care of those little Negroes left at home, and they had to go eat a bite. They would come back for the wake.

Already a few tables and chairs, borrowed from the neighborhood, had been installed in the yard. An aroma of coffee and cinnamon tea was spreading. Laurélien lent two *gourdes*, all he had, so that they might buy some *clairin*. Délira had barely enough to pay the *Père Savane* who would come to read the prayers and bless the body. They hadn't the wherewithal for a church funeral. That was too expensive, and the church extends no credit to the poor. It's not a shop—it's God's house.

The weeping quieted down. Night came with its weight of shadow and silence. From time to time, a woman sighed, "Ah, Jesus-Mary-Virgin!" but not with much conviction. In the long run folks tire even of grief.

Délira sat next to Manuel. She did not take her eyes from him, and at times she seemed to be whispering to him. No one heard what she was saying. Annaise left. She went to explain things to Rosanna. That wouldn't be easy. Bienaimé was still in the same place, his head in his folded arms resting on his knees. Was he asleep? They didn't know. Nobody disturbed him.

Laurélien was busy making a coffin in front of his hut with saw and hammer. Anselme, his younger brother, held a torch of candlewood. It was not a big job—three planks and a lid to entrust to the earth this man who had been his friend.

What a man Manuel was! he mused. What a peasant! There wasn't his better in the whole country. But death made its choice like a blind man who selects mangoes at the mart, groping until he finds a good one and leaving the bad. That's the truth—and it's not right.

"Pass me the nails," he said to Anselme.

His movements were silhouetted on the wall of the hut by huge deformed shadows. Anselme was just on the threshold of manhood. If he repeated Manuel's words to him, perhaps he wouldn't understand. I used to watch him weave those hats, his fingers would run through the straw, and he'd say, "A day will come—we'll make a great *coumbite* of all the farmers to clear out poverty and plant a new life." You won't see that day, Chief, you've gone before your time, but you've left us hope and courage.

One more nail, one more. Bring the light closer, Anselme, one more nail. The coffin is finished. The lid fits. I've finished, and to tell the truth, Brother Manuel, it's a job for which I deserved no thanks.

He looked at his work—a long plain box. The wood was too thin, too green. The earth would eat it up in no time. If only I'd been able to get a few good mahogany planks, and maybe some iron bindings like those that *M'sieur* Paulma sells in town, but those are dear, out of reach.

"They've started with the canticles," Anselme said.

"I hear," Lauréilien replied.

The chant rose sadly from the heart of the night:

By what excessive kindness Thou hast taken upon Thyself the weight of our crimes. Thou hast suffered cruel death to save us from death.

When it wavered, a woman's voice, high and vibrant, somewhat cracked, took it up again, uniting the other voices, and the canticle started anew in unanimous transport.

It was time to go to the wake.

In the front room of the hut, Délira arranged on a tablecloth a crucifix, lighted candles, and such flowers as could be found in all the drought.

And now, Lord, Thou lettest Thy servant depart in peace, according to Thy word.

The peasants droned their canticles before the altar, crowded one against the other, and the light from the candles made shiny reflections on their black sweaty faces.

Fortunately, there was *clairin* to cool them off. Antoine had consumed more than a reasonable amount. Already he was no longer very firm on his legs, but was singing at the top of his lungs. When he let his harsh, powerful voice ring out, it covered that of the others. Destine, with all apparent innocence, jabbed her elbow in the pit of his stomach, and a hiccough almost choked him.

"The shameless wench!" he exclaimed a moment later in the yard. "She doesn't even respect the dead Manuel." Then in a menacing tone, "That's all right. I'll make up a song about her, damn it, that'll—" But he remembered that he was at a wake, so he swallowed the enormous obscenity that was on the very tip of his tongue.

On each table, they had placed a candle that created the illusion of little islands of light in the yard. Peasants sat round playing *trois-sept*. They held their cards like fans, and seemed absorbed. Had they already forgotten Manuel?

Oh, no! You mustn't think that! Only, men can't go around crying like women. That soothes the womenfolks, but a man has courage enough to bear grief in silence. Besides, it's the custom to play cards at wakes.

"Nine of diamonds. I cut."

Bienaimé was like a body without a soul. He entered the room where Manuel reposed. He looked down for a moment with deep empty eyes. He went out in the yard and walked past the tables. They spoke to him. He didn't answer. After much prayer and pleading, Délira made him eat a little stew, but he left almost all of it on his plate.

"He's like a man struck by lightning!" Antoine said. "He's done in."

Annaise returned. She had explained to Rosanna. Rosanna had screamed and called her all sorts of names.

"Aren't you ashamed?" she cried.

"No," Annaise answered.

"You're a common woman if ever there was one," Rosanna shouted, "a woman without conscience, without honor!"

"No," Annaise replied, "I'm his wife. He was the finest man on earth. He was honest and he was kind. He didn't fool me or take me by violence. I'm the one who wanted it . . ."

"But how did you manage to meet him, enemies that we are?"

"He loved me and I loved him. Our paths crossed."

She took off her silver earrings. She put on her black dress and, on her head, a white kerchief.

"You're not going out!" Rosanna stood before the door.

"I'm in grief, mama," Annaise said.

"So much the worse! I say you're not going out!"

"I'm in sorrow, mama," said Annaise.

"You heard me. I won't repeat it three times."

Someone knocked on the door. It was Gille. Gille entered and saw what was going on.

"Gervilen was right," he remarked. "You and Manuel were accomplices." He paused. "Early this morning, Gervilen left Fonds Rouge."

Annaise said nothing. She remembered her oath.

"Do you know where the water is?" Gille asked.

"I know where it is," Annaise replied.

"Let her go out, mama," said Gille. Annaise went out.

You have to pass the time away somehow at wakes. Cards, hymns, and white rum don't suffice, the night is long.

Near the kitchen, Antoine, a cup of coffee in his hand, was telling riddles. Those who surrounded him were mostly young folks. Not that the older peasants wouldn't enjoy it, but it didn't seem quite proper, especially when you value your reputation as a grave, stern man. Suppose you were forced to laugh at some of Antoine's unexpected sallies? Then what? Then these young Negroes would have no more respect for you—they're always ready to consider you their equal and their pal, those little monkeys!

Antoine began: "On entering the house, all the women take off their dresses."

The others tried to guess, digging deep into their imaginations. Oh, pshaw! They couldn't find the answer.

"What is it?" Anselme asked.

"The schooners clew up their sails on entering port," explained Antoine. He swallowed a drink of coffee.

"I'm going to the king's. I find two roads and have to take them both."

"A pair of pants!" exclaimed Lazare.

"That's right. But this one—my name isn't Antoine if you get it—Little Marie put her fist on her hip and said, 'I'm a big girl.' "

"That's hard, *oui*, that's hard."

"You aren't intelligent enough. Bunch of thick-skulled Negroes that you are!"

They tried and tried in vain, then gave up. Antoine triumphed.

"A cup!" He held his cup by the handle, showed it to them and laughed for joy.

"Another one, Uncle Antoine, just one more," they pleaded in chorus.

"Shhh!" You're making too much noise! Looks like you can't get enough!"

He pretended that he had to be begged, but he was only too happy to keep on, Antoine was. All over the plain they could tell you that no one was more famous for his tales and songs.

"Good!" he said. "I'm going to make this one easy for you. Round as a ball, long as the high road."

"A spool of thread."

"I burn my tongue and give my blood to please society."

"A lamp."

"My coat is green, my shirt is white, my pants are red, my tie is black."

"A watermelon."

"Anselme, my boy," said Antoine, "go and fill this cup with *clairin*, up to the brim, you hear? You mustn't spare the *clairin* at a wake. You've got to do honor to the dead. If Sister Destine has the bottle, just tell her it's for Laurélien. Just as a precaution, son, just as a precaution—because that Destine and I, we get along like milk and lemons. We get sick at the stomach merely from looking at each other."

That's how the wake proceeded, between tears and laughter. Just like life, brother. *Oui*, exactly like life.

A small group formed to one side. Old Dorélien Jean-Jacques, Fleurimond Fleury, Dieuveille Riché, and Laurélien Laurore.

"In my opinion," Dorélien said, "it's a death that isn't natural."

"That's what I think myself," Fleurimond approved.

Laurélien didn't share this opinion. "Délira said it was the bad fevers. If she said so, that's the way it is. She'd have no reason to lie. And there are fevers that consume you without seeming to. We're like a piece of furniture that looks very solid, very strong, but the termites are already inside. And one fine day, we fall into dust."

"Maybe so," said Fleurimond. But he didn't seem too convinced.

Then Dieuveille Riché took the floor. "At noon you cross the river on foot. Dry, not *that* much water, just pebbles and rocks. But the rain has fallen like an avalanche in the mountains, and in the afternoon, the water descends like a mad beast and ravages everything as it passes in its fury. That's how death comes, when we least expect it. And there's nothing we can do to prevent it, brothers."

"About the water," Laurélien said, "it remains to be seen whether Manuel told anyone where the spring is. I was his friend, but he didn't have time to show me the spot."

"Maybe Délira knows."

"More probably Rosanna's daughter does."

"Because it would be the worst luck we could have if he had gone with the secret."

"We'd have to scour the entire countryside, searching the smallest cracks of the hills and ravines."

"And even then, you couldn't be sure of finding it."

"We had built up our hopes, and in advance we could see all these fields irrigated. It would be a pity."

"For tough luck, that would really be tough luck. I was already planning to plant beans on one edge of my field. Beans are bringing in a good price nowadays at the market."

"And bananas could grow by the canal."

"I," Dieuveille said, "I was going to try leeks and tropical onions on my piece of land."

Old Dorélien sighed. "So each Negro had his plans. One said, 'I'll do this.' The other said, 'I'll do that.' And all the while, misfortune was laughing on the sly, and waiting at the turn of the road we call Death. Ah, I am going, *mes amis*, I am going, *oui*. I haven't much time left, but I would like to see the cornfields green once more and the crops covering the fields."

> *Forward into com . . . bat,*
> *On to glo . . . ry!*

They're tough, those hymn singers, they don't easily get out of breath. Fat Destine, conquered by fatigue, had plopped down in a chair. Her head rocked on her shoulders, her eyes closed, but she was still beating time with her bare foot, and singing in a sad, sleepy falsetto.

"Ugh! she's ugly!" Antoine whispered with a wry look of disgust.

The bottle of white rum was on the table. He reached for it, but Destine opened one eye, just one—but it was firm, and Antoine pretended to be snuffing out a candle.

"That's just wasting wax," he explained. And he withdrew, his shoulders stooped, swearing between his teeth in words that could not be repeated.

> *Forward in . . . to com . . . bat,*
> *On to glo. . .oo. . .ry!*

Destine sang, but this time in a clarion, triumphant tone which injected new life into the choir as a fresh log revives a fire. Their song was wafted away on the trembling wings of dawn. The peasants who rose early in Fonds Rouge heard it.

"Ah! yes," they said, "the funeral's today."

And those who were sleeping under the arbor with their heads on the table, woke up and asked for coffee. Délira hadn't left Manuel for a second, nor had poor Annaise. Bienaimé had curled up in a corner.

It was the last hymn, the very last, for day came with black chilly trees against a pale sky, and the peasants began to take leave. They would come back later. They disappeared over the paths under the thorn acacias, and the wild guinea hens came down from the branches and assembled in the clearings. Roosters strained their throats from yard to yard, and a young colt neighed nervously on the savanna.

"*Adieu*, Délira," Laurélien said. He hesitated. "*Adieu* Annaise."

They answered him in a weak voice, for they had wept too much, they had no more strength.

Dawn came in through the window, but Manuel would never see it again. He had gone to sleep for always and forever.

Amen!

About ten o'clock, Aristomène, the *Père Savane*, made his entrance in the courtyard. He was riding a little donkey which bent under his weight and the old man's feet were dragging in the dust. He was late and the animal was restive. Aristomène dug his heels in its flanks so vigorously that he almost lifted it from the ground. He was wearing a long cloak that must have been black once upon a time, but, because of its great age, now bordered onto the glistening color of a wood pigeon's throat. With an unctuous gesture, he removed his hat and revealed a shiny bald head.

"*Bonjour*, one and all!"

The peasants greeted him politely. They offered him a seat, and Délira in person served him a cup of coffee. Aristomène drank slowly. He was conscious of his importance as the murmur of conversation buzzed about him like a homage. His reddish pockmarked face sweated in abundant satisfaction.

In the house, they had placed Manuel in his coffin. Two candles burned, one at his head, the other at his feet. Bienaimé gazed at his son. He was not weeping, but his mouth couldn't stop trembling. It wasn't certain that he had seen Annaise. Her hands covered her face. The tears streamed through her fingers and she sobbed like a hurt child.

Every now and then, some sister—Clairemise, Mérila, Destine, Célina, Irézile or Georgiana, or some other—uttered a strident scream and all immediately accompanied her, and the mourners' chorus filled the hut with deafening cries.

The men stood in the yard or on the porch. They talked in a low voice, biting the stems of their pipes. But Laurélien was in the room with death.

"Goodbye, Chief. I'll never have another friend like you! *Adieu*, my brother! *Adieu*, comrade!"

He wiped his eyes on the back of his hand. It wasn't usual to see a black man cry, but he couldn't help it and he was not ashamed.

Délira had returned to her post near the coffin. She fanned Manuel's face with one of those straw hats that he used to weave in the afternoon on the porch. She was protecting him from the flies, from the fat flies that are seen only at funerals. The flickering candlelight illumined Manuel's brow.

"There was a light on your forehead the day you came back from Cuba, and not even death can take it away. You're carrying it into the shadows with you. May this light in your soul guide you through everlasting night, so that you can find the road to that country of Guinea where you'll rest in peace with the wise men of our people."

"We're about to start," said Aristomène. He was perusing his book, wetting a finger to turn each page.

"Prayer for the dead."

The women fell on their knees. Délira opened wide her arms, her eyes raised toward something only she could see.

"From the depth of the abyss, I have cried to Thee, Lord! Lord, hear my voice. May Thine ears be attentive to the voice of my prayer!"

He read at top speed, Aristomène did. He swallowed his words without chewing them, he was in such a hurry. Brother Hilarion had invited him to have a drink after the ceremony. And for these measly two *gourdes* and a half that he was going to be paid, this was not worth bothering much about. No, it was really not worth the trouble.

"*May they rest in peace. Amen.*"

"Amen," the peasants repeated.

Aristomène sponged his skull, his face, and his neck with a wide checked handkerchief. Notwithstanding his haste, he enjoyed the Latin words that he was going to utter. Those "*vobiscums, saeculums,* and *dominums*" that sounded like a stick falling on a drum, and that made these ignorant peasants prattle with admiration.

"My! but he's smart, *oui*, that Aristomène!"

His voice rose in the plaintive, nasal, solemn drawl of a priest. It wasn't for nothing that he had been a sexton for years. And if it hadn't been for that regrettable affair with the Father's housekeeper, he'd still be serving mass at the town church. Oh, that hadn't been his fault. Father should have chosen an older woman to be his servant instead of some young *Négresse*, plump and round as a bantam chicken.

"*Lead us not into temptation,*" the Scripture says.

If words had bones, Aristomène would have choked, he was hurrying so. The pages flew under his fingers as he turned several at a time.

"There's a slick Negro for you!" reflected Antoine, watching him closely.

Délira heard this hurried language, this sacred gibberish, only as a distant, incomprehensible rumbling. She sat beside Manuel. She saw him alone. And she swayed on her chair as if she were exhausted from bearing her burden of sorrow. She was like a branch in a storm, abandoned to a bitter, endless night.

"Pardon, pardon, I ask pardon and deliverance, Lord, take me for I am tired! Old Délira is so, so tired! Lord, let me accompany my boy into that great savanna of death. Let me wade with him across that river in the country of the dead. I carried him for nine months in my body and for a whole lifetime in my heart. I can't leave him!

"Manuel, ah, Manuel! You were my two eyes, you were my blood. I saw with your eyes like the night sees with the stars. I breathed through your mouth, and my veins opened when your blood flowed. Your wound wounded me. Your death killed me. I've nothing more to do on earth. All that's left for me is to wait in some corner of life like an old rag forgotten at the foot of a wall, like a poor helpless woman who holds out her hand. 'Charity, please,' she says. But the charity she asks is death.

"Hail Mary, Gracious Virgin! Make that day come! Make it come tomorrow! Make it come today even! Oh, my saints, oh, my *loas*, come and help me! Papa Legba, I call you! St. Joseph, papa, I call you! Dambala Siligoué, I call you! Ogoun Shango, I call you! St. James the Elder, I call you! Ah! Loko Atisou, papa! Ay, Guéde Hounsou, I call you! Agoueta Royo Doko Agoué, I call on you! My boy is dead. He's going away. He's going across the sea. He's going to Guinea. *Adieu, adieu,* I say *adieu* to my boy. He'll never come back. He's gone forever. Ah, my sadness! My heartbreak! My misery! My grief!"

She lifted her arms to heaven, her face disfigured by tears and suffering, her shoulders rocked by this desperate incantation. The womenfolks supported her and whispered, "Courage, Délira, dear! Be brave!"

But she didn't hear them, she didn't hear Aristomène as he chanted faster and faster, hurrying to get through.

"*Santae Trinitatis. Per Christum Dominum Nostrum. Amen!*"

Then from the depths of his cloak he took out a small bottle. He pulled out the stopper with his teeth and sprinkled the body with holy water, and Laurélien came forward with the coffin lid.

"No, no!" Annaise cried, struggling in Clairemise's arms, but Laurélien drew nearer with the lid.

"Let me see him for the last time," Délira cried.

But Laurélien nailed down the lid, and with each blow of the hammer Délira trembled as though the nails were being driven into her soul.

It's over, yes, it's over. Joachim, Dieuveille, Fleurimond, and Laurélien lifted up the coffin. There were wails and groans and voices that cried, "Help me, O God!" for the tall Negroes were carrying the coffin away. They were carrying their brother off toward that earth that he loved so much and for which he had died.

They walked slowly toward the edge of the thorn acacias, and the cortège of peasants followed them. The women were weeping and the men walked in silence. They had dug the grave in the shade of a logwood tree. A pair of turtledoves flew off with a frightened trembling of their wings and were lost beyond the fields in the noonday sun.

"Let him down easy," Laurélien said. The coffin slipped downward to rest at the bottom of the hole.

"Poor devil!" Antoine said. "He died in the bloom of his youth and he was a good fellow, this Manuel."

Laurélien and Fleurimond seized the shovels. A stone rolled down and struck against the coffin. Earth flowed into the grave. The coffin began to disappear. Stifled sobs were heard and the dull thud of clods of earth hardened by the drought. The hole began to fill.

A woman groaned, "God, we ask Thee for strength and courage, consolation and resignation."

Manuel wasn't a partisan of resignation, Laurélien reflected. The signs of the cross, and all this kneeling, and "Lord, Good Lord," he said, meant nothing—that a man was made for rebellion. Now you're dead, Chief, dead and buried. But your words we won't forget. And, if, one day on the hard road of this life, weariness should tempt us with, "What's the use?" and "It's not worth the trouble," we'll hear your voice and we'll be of good courage.

With one hand, Laurélien wiped away the sweat that covered his face. He leaned both hands on the handle of his shovel. The grave was filled.

"Well, it's finished," Antoine said. "May you find rest, Brother Manuel, in that eternity of eternities!"

"In eternity," the others answered.

The circle of peasants broke up. They returned to the hut to tell Délira and Bienaimé *au revoir*. Then, since folks get thirsty under the hot sun, they went to get a little drink—that could only do them good—one last drink of white rum.

"How about it, neighbor?"

But Laurélien remained. He fashioned a little mound of dirt above the grave. Around it he placed some big stones. When they had enough money, he'd build a tomb of brick with a niche where they could light candles in his memory. Then on a plaque of fresh cement, Antoine, since he knew how, would write in a slow painstaking hand:

HERE LAYS MANUEL JAN-JOSEF

Chapter Fourteen

THE VERY EVENING of the burial, Délira went to Larivoire's. She knocked on his door.

"Who's there?" Larivoire asked. He was already in bed.

"It's me—Délira, me."

Stopping just long enough to light the lamp, Larivoire let her in.

"Respect, neighbor," he said "Come in, please."

Délira sat down. She arranged the folds of her black dress. She was straight and stern.

"You were expecting me, Larivoire?"

"I was expecting you." There was a silence between them. "Gervilen," Larivoire said without looking at her.

"I know," she replied. "But no one will ever find out. I mean, Hilarion, the authorities."

"Manuel didn't want them to?"

" 'No, no,' he said, as he struggled on his deathbed. 'We've got to save the water,' he kept repeating. He held my hand."

Larivoire raised the wick of the lamp. "He came here the same night of the trouble. He stood under that arbor in the midst of the peasants. He was speaking. I looked at him. I listened to him. I know a man when I see one. He was a Negro of great quality."

"He's dead," Délira said.

"You have a heavy grief to bear, sister."

"My sorrow is great," Délira answered.

Larivoire scratched his chin, pulled on the hair of his beard. "Did he entrust you with a mission?"

"Yes, and that's why I'm here. Go get your folks, Larivoire."

"It's late," the other said.

"My words need the night. Go get your folks, Larivoire."

Larivoire got up, took a few hesitant steps about the room. "Was it your dead Manuel who asked you to talk to them?"

"Yes, it was he. But I, too, want to. I've got my reasons."

Larivoire took his hat. "We've got to respect the will of the dead," he said. He half opened the door. "You won't have to wait too long. I'm going to stop by my son Similien's. He'll notify some and I'll notify the others. If the lamp burns down, lift the wick. It's not a bad lamp, but the kerosene that Florentine sells is no good."

Délira remained alone. Her head dropped down on her breast, and she folded her hands. The light flickered, the room was peopled by shadows. She closed her eyes.

"I'm worn out! Délira's worn out. She can't go on, *mes amis!*"

Weariness was dragging her into an eddy, to the verge of a fainting spell, slow and irresistible like nausea. But the thought of Manuel buoyed her up.

"I've got to talk to those folks. Afterward I'll go to bed. To sleep, ah, to sleep! And if the day should break without me, it would be, to tell the honest truth, a day of mercy."

"You stayed in the dark all this time!" Larivoire exclaimed. The lamp had gone out. He fumbled in his pocket and finally found the matches. "They're outside, *oui*," he said.

"Bring the lamp nearer. I want to see their faces." The room lighted up—the table, a demijohn on the oak buffet, a mat rolled up in a corner, and on the whitewashed wall, pictures of saints, an old almanac.

"Let them come in," Délira said.

Délira stood up in her long dress of mourning.

"Close the door!" she ordered.

Louisimé Jean-Pierre shut the door. Slowly Délira looked at them. She seemed to be counting them one by one and, as her sad stern gaze reached them, they would lower their heads.

"I don't see Gervilen. I say that I don't see Gervilen Gervilis. I'm asking where is Gervilis?"

In the silence, you distinctly heard the heavy breathing of the peasants.

"Because I would have liked to repeat my boy's words to Gervilen Gervilis. He told me, here's what Manuel, my boy, told me. 'You've offered sacrifices to the *loas*, you've offered the blood of chickens and young goats to make the rain fall. All that has been useless. Because what counts is the sacrifice of a man, the blood of a man.' "

"That's a great word, *oui*," said Larivoire, nodding his head gravely.

"He also told me, 'Go and find Larivoire. Tell him the wish of my blood that has been spilled—reconciliation, reconciliation!' He said it twice. 'So that life can begin anew, so the day can break on the dew.' And I wanted to send word to Hilarion, but he was holding my hand. 'No, no,' he said, and the black blood was running from his mouth. 'The water would be lost. We've got to save the water!' "

"Délira," said Larivoire in a hoarse voice, and he wiped his eyes with his closed fist, "it's been seventy-seven years since water flowed from my eyes, but I tell you, in truth, your boy was a real man, a peasant to the roots of his soul! We won't see another like him soon."

"Mama," said Nérestan in a strangely tender voice, "you've had a great sorrow, mama."

"Yes, son," Délira answered, "and I thank you for your sympathy. But I didn't come here to tell you about my grief. I came to bring you the last wish of my son. He was talking to me, but he was really talking to all of you, 'Sing my mourning,' he said, 'sing my mourning with a song of the *coumbite*!' "

It's customary to sing mourning with hymns for the dead, but he, Manuel had chosen a hymn for the living—the chant of the *coumbite*, the chant of the soil, of the water, the plants, of friendship between peasants, because he wanted his death to be the beginning of life for you.

Peasants are hard and tough. Life has tanned their hearts. But they only seem to be thick and rude. You've got to know them—for no one is more blessed with those qualities that give a man the right to call himself a man—kindness, bravery, true brotherhood.

And Larivoire spoke for them all when he approached Délira, his hand extended, and trembling with emotion.

"Take this hand, Délira, and with it our promise and our word of honor." He turned toward the peasants. "Is that true?"

"Yes," the peasants replied.

"Peace and reconciliation?"

And Nérestan advanced. "Mama, I'll dig the canal in your fields myself."

"I'll plant them for you, Délira," said Josaphat.

"Count on me, too," Louisimé added.

"And I'll weed out your plot any time it needs it," said Similien.

"I'll be there," Gille promised.

"We'll all be there," the others assured her.

Over Délira's face there passed a semblance of gentleness. "Thanks, my friends, for this consolation. My boy hears you in his grave. This is how he wanted it—one family of peasants united in friendship. My part has ended.

"Only," and she regained her severity, "only we're accomplices from today on—I didn't come here, you understand? And it was the bad fevers that killed Manuel. Do you understand me fully? Make the sign of the cross on your lips."

They obeyed.

"Swear!"

The peasants struck their chests three times just over the heart, and raised their hands for the oath.

"We swear," they said.

For a moment, Délira studied their faces. Yes, they were good peasant stock, simple, frank, honest.

"Larivoire, my brother," she said, "let another week pass. We've got to respect the mourning. Then you'll come with them to Laurélien's after sunrise. My folks will be expecting you. And then, Annaise, my daughter-in-law, will lead you all to the stream. She knows the place. The wood pigeons flap their wings in its foliage. Oh, fiddlesticks! There I go talking nonsense! It's because I'm so tired, *mes amis.* This old Délira, as you see, has no more strength, no, not a bit. So I bid you good night, *oui.*"

Louisimé Jean-Pierre opened the door for her.

"Wait," said Larivoire, "Similien's going to take you home."

"No, Larivoire, no. That's not necessary. Thanks just the same. There's a moon, the stars are shining. I'll see my way."

And she went out in the dark.

The End
And The Beginning

BIENAIMÉ DOZED UNDER the calabash tree. The little dog lay in front of the kitchen, his head between his paws. From time to time he opened one eye to snap at a fly. Délira was mending a dress. She held the material close to her eyes, for her sight was getting bad. The sun went its rounds, high in the sky, and the day ran through all the others.

Things had fallen back into the old routine, they'd returned to the beaten path. Each week, Délira went to sell charcoal at the market. Laurélien chopped the wood and prepared the charcoal pit for her. He was a good boy, Laurélien.

Bienaimé had changed so you wouldn't recognize him. Formerly the slightest contradiction used to make him boil. He was always on the verge of anger and irritation, always ready with a retort. A real gamecock! Now, a spring had broken inside him. He said, "*Oui*" to everything like a child. Just, "Yes," and "All right."

Délira had caught him several times in Manuel's room, his hand patting the empty place in the bed and tears streaming into his white beard. Every morning he went to the grave at the edge of the thorn acacias. They had sheltered it under a little arbor of palm leaves. He squatted down near it and smoked his pipe, his gaze vague and distant. He would stay there for hours if Délira didn't come looking for him to take him to the shade of the calabash tree. He'd follow her docilely. He slept a lot and at any time of the day. Antoine was right, he was like a man struck by lightning.

From afar the wind brought a squall of voices and an untiring drumbeat. For more than a month, the peasants had been working at a *coumbite*. They'd dug a canal, a deep gully from the spring to Fonds Rouge, across the narrow plain through the acacia trees, and they'd joined it to their fields by small ditches.

Rage almost strangled Hilarion. Ah, you can imagine how furious he became. And now Florentine nagged from morning till night, as if it were his fault, browbeating him with all kinds of reproaches. Could *he* have foreseen that Manuel was going to die? Naturally, he should have arrested him in time, for they could have made him tell where the spring was located—they had ways of making them talk. The lieutenant had called him an imbecile. Now Florentine—you could hear her harsh voice all over Fonds Rouge. When he had had enough, Hilarion would make her feel the weight of his heavy copper beltbuckle. That calmed her down more or less, the bitch!

Perhaps, he thought, perhaps I could ask Judge Sainville, the Communal Magistrate, to put a tax on that water. I'd get my share and lay it aside. We'll see about that.

But would the peasants stand for it? They had been working lately right by the spring itself, at the very head of the water. They had followed Manuel's instructions point by point. He was dead, Manuel, but he was still guiding them.

Someone entered Déilira's yard, a tall *Négresse*, a beautiful *Négresse*. It was Annaise. The old woman saw her coming and her heart was glad.

"*Bonjour, mama*," said Annaise.

"Eh, *bonjour*, daughter," Délira replied.

"You're going to ruin your eyes," said Annaise. "Let me mend that dress for you."

"It's simply that it keeps me occupied, daughter. I sew, I sew—and I stitch the old days and the new. If only we could mend life, Anna, and catch up the broken threads! Oh, God! We can't!"

"Manuel said—I can still hear him, as though it were yesterday—he said to me, 'Life is a thread that doesn't break, that is never lost, and do you know why? Because every man ties a knot in it during his lifetime with the work he has done. That's what keeps life going through the centuries—man's work on this earth.' "

"My boy was a Negro who thought deep," said Délira proudly.

Snatches of the song reached their ears. It sounded a bit like *Hoho Ehhé Ohkoenhého,* and the drum was jubilant. It stammered with joy, for Antoine was handling it with more skill than ever.

"Gille told me they're going to turn the water into the canal today. Suppose we went and looked, mama? It's a great event, *oui.*"

"As you wish, dear."

Délira got up. Her shoulders had bent a bit and she had become even drier than before.

"The sun's hot. I'm going to put on my hat." But already Annaise was running to the hut to get it for her.

"You're obliging, daughter," Délira thanked her. And she smiled that smile that had kept all the gracefulness of youth despite the small scars of sadness with which life marked the corners of her lips.

They went into the woods along the road Manuel had followed the day after his arrival. The acacias smelled like the tepid smoke of the charcoal pits. They walked silently until they came out into a valley inundated by light. The arborescent cactus stood erect with their wide hairy leaves of a dull and dusty green.

"Look!" Annaise exclaimed, "Folks are right to call them 'donkey ears!' They seem so crabby and stubborn and mean, those plants do."

"Plants are like humans—they come in two classes, good and bad. When you see oranges, all those little suns hanging up in the leaves, you feel a rejoicing. They're nice and they're useful, oranges are. While, take a plant with prickles like that one—but we mustn't curse anything. The Good Lord created everything."

"And the calabash," said Annaise, "it looks like a man's head and it's wrapped around something white like a brain—yet it's a stupid fruit. You can't eat it."

"My, you're bright, *oui!*" Délira cried. "You're going to make old Délira laugh in spite of herself."

They went up toward Fanchon Mound. Délira walked slowly because of her age. Annaise came along behind her. The path was rather steep, but luckily it took a few turns.

"I won't go as far as the plateau," Délira said. "Here's a big rock just made, you might say, for a bench."

The two women sat down. The plain lay at their feet in the burning noon. On their left, they saw the huts of Fonds Rouge and the rusty patches of their enclosed fields. The savanna spread below them like an esplanade of violent light. But across the plain the vein of the canal ran toward the thorn acacias which had been cleared along the route for its passage. And if you had good eyes, you could see a line of ditches already prepared in the fields.

"That's where they are," said Annaise, stretching her arm toward a wooded hill. "That's where they're working."

The drum rose exultantly. Its rapid beat echoed over the plain. And the men were singing:

> *Manuel Jean-Joseph, Oh!*
> *Mighty Negro! Enhého!*

"You hear, mama?"

"I hear," Délira said.

Soon this arid plain would be covered with high grass. In the fields banana trees, corn, sweet potatoes, yams, red and white laurel would be growing. And it would be thanks to her son.

The song suddenly stopped.

"What's happening?" Délira asked.

"I don't know, no."

Then an enormous clamor burst out. The women rose. The peasants came into view running from the mountain, throwing their hats into the air. They were dancing and kissing each other.

"Mama," said Annaise, in a strangely weak voice, "there's the water."

A thin thread of water advanced, flowing through the plain, and the peasants went along with it, shouting and singing. Antoine led them proudly beating his drum.

"Oh, Manuel! Manuel! Manuel! Why are you dead?" Délira groaned.

"No," said Annaise. She smiled through her tears. "No, he isn't dead."

She took the old woman's hand and pressed it gently against her belly where the new life was stirring.

Glossary

Atibon Legba (Papa Legba), Agoué, Ashadé Bôkô, Batala, Bolada Kimalada, Kataroulo, Papa Loko, Papa Ogoun, Olicha Baguita Wanguita: Afro-Haitian deities termed *loas*, venerated among the peasants as are also the saints of the Catholic Church. Catholic and Vodun deities sometimes merge and take on a single identity. During the ceremonies, these may be impersonated by living worshipers.

Abobo! Ago yé!: Religious exclamations of ecstasy.

Asogwê: An Afro-Haitian religious ritual.

Bueno: Spanish word meaning good.

Cacos: Peasant revolutionaries.

Carajo, caramba: Mild Cuban oaths.

Chandelier: A cactus tree similar to the Joshua tree or buckthorn, planted as a barrier between plots of land.

Clairin: A raw white rum.

Coumbite: A collective agricultural effort in which neighboring farmers help each other at times such as the harvest, when a task requires more hands than a single peasant family affords.

Creole (Krèyol): The language of the Haitian peasant, an Afro-Creole language. There is sometimes, especially in his serious moments, a quality of dignity and grandeur in the Haitian peasant's speech, giving it an almost biblical flavor, to a certain extent due to many archaic words and expressions from the old French of Napoleon's day that are still a part of his language.

Cric?... Crac!: Conventional form of beginning a story. The narrator says, "Cric?" and the listener replies, "Crac!"

Gourde: A monetary unit, approximately twenty cents.

Honor! . . . Respect!: A form of salutation. Before entering a peasant's hut one says, *"Honneur!"* The peasant replies, *"Respect!"*

Houngan: Vodun priest.

Hounsi: Vodun priest's assistants..

Père Savane: Bush priest who recites Catholic prayers. Often he is also a helper at Vodun ceremonies. In many cases the peasants cannot afford a regular priest and, in the outlying districts, there may not be a priest available.

Malanga: A bulbous plant with wide leaves like elephant ears.

Nègre, Négresse: In the French- and Spanish-speaking Caribbean islands these words often have a connotation of affection, entirely non-racial in meaning. *Mon Nègre, ma petite Négresse*, is equivalent to, *My dear, my darling, my sweet.*

Simidor: One who leads a group of men at work by setting the pace with song and drum.

Tafia: Rum.

Urine that spreads doesn't foam: A Haitian proverb equivalent to, "A rolling stone gathers no moss."

Yanvalou: A slow religious dance.

The novel was translated into many languages including:

Czech: Vlàdcovia vlahy Prague, Nakladatelstvi-Svoboda, 1948.

Danish: Duggens Herrer (Helga Vang Laurisden), Copenhague, Fremad, 1950.

Dutch: Dauwdruppels op Haïti (Tilly Visser), Amsterdam, Pegasus, 1950.

English: Masters of the Dew (Langston Hughes & Mercer Cook), New York, Reynal & Hitchcock, 1947.

German: Herr über den Tau (Eva Klemperer), Zürich, Universum Verlag, 1948.

Greek: Hoi aphentes tou nerou, Athena, Kedros, 1960.

Hungarian: Fekete Emberek (Peter Komoly), Budapest, Révail, 1950.

Hebrew: Sarha Talalium, Sifriat Poalim, Ltd., Worker's Book Guild (Hashomer Hatzair) State of Israel, 1948.

Italian: Il giorno sorge sull'acqua, Rome, Instituto editoriale italiano, 1948

Lithuanian: Rasos Seimininkai (J. Naujokaitis), Vilnius, Goslitizdat, 1959.

Polish: Zródlo, powiesc (Hanna Oledzka), Varsovie, Panstwowy Instytut Wydawniczy, 1949.

Portuguese: Os Donos do carvalho (Emmo Duarte) Rio de Janeiro, Vitoria, 1955.

Romanian: Stadinii Apelor (Vlad Musatescu),

Bucarest, Editura Pentru literatura universala, 1965.

Russian: Khoziaeva rosy, Moscou, Inostrannaia literatura, 1956.

Serbo-croate: Gospodari Rose (Emilija Andjelic), Belgrade, Novo pokolenje, 1951.

Spanish: Gobernantes del rocío (Fina Warschaver), Buenos Aires, Lautaro, 1951.

Vietnamese: Dân dát suong dêm (Lê Trong Bông), Hanoï, Lao Bong, 1980.

Order Form

2725 NW 19th. Street
Pompano Beach, Fl. 33069
Tel.: 954-968.7433   Fax: 954-970.0330
e-mail: caribbeanstudiespress@earthlink.net
www.caribbeanstudiespress.com

Name:_____

Address:_____

_____ Telephone:_____

Please send the following:

Quantity	Title	Price $	Sub-Total
	Masters of the Dew	19.50	
	Tax (6% for Florida Residents)		
	Shipping 10% of Total (Minimum $6.90)		

Please make check payable to:
Educa Vision Inc.
We accept Visa and Master Card

TOTAL [   ]

You might also be interested in:

Cat.#: B123

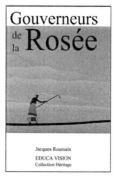

Cat.#: B075